THE *Abalone* SHELL

Books by Suzie O'Connell

www.suzieoconnell.com

THE *Abalone* SHELL

Sea Glass Cove

BOOK ONE

Suzie O'Connell

SUNSET
Rose
BOOKS

ISBN-10: 1545384533
ISBN-13: 978-1545384534

In loving memory of Jenny Ferguson.
Happy 101st birthday, Grandma.

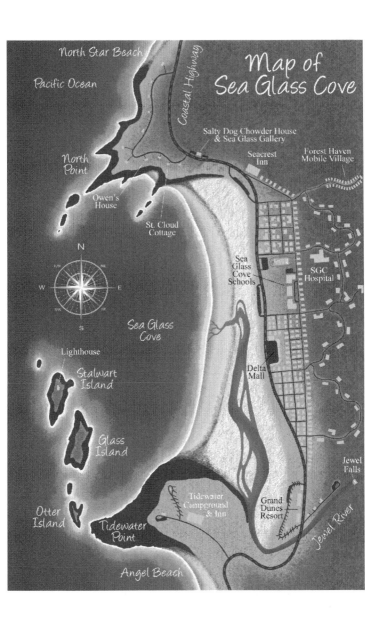

One

IF DIVORCING HER HUSBAND was the best decision she'd made in the last year, spending the summer at her family's clifftop cottage in Sea Glass Cove was the second best. From her vantage point on the back deck, Hope had a spectacular view of the cove, the mile-long beach, and the town, and the islands and sea stacks that sheltered it all from the Pacific Ocean. Waves pounded the rocky bluffs in a ceaseless rhythm that filled the thick coastal air with salt spray, and her lips curved in a slow smile.

The cottage was one of eleven houses perched on the rocky point that marked the northern boundary of Sea Glass Cove. Half-hidden by the native, wind-stunted cedars and firs that dotted the point, it was sided like the rest of the houses on North Point with weather-grayed cedar shakes that further helped it disappear into the vegetation. With the houses spaced far apart, it was always quiet and private up here, and Hope was looking forward to using that peace to find a new routine for her life. She loved her home in Montana, but Dan's presence lingered everywhere, and so far, she hadn't been able to focus on the future.

She turned her back on the cove and ocean and took in the familiar angles of the home her grandfather had built. There were so many cherished memories here, unblemished by the shadow of her marriage, and among them were all the pieces she needed to start the healing process. In August, when it was time to go home, she'd be able to do it with a clear head.

"Well?" she asked, glancing down at her seven-year-old daughter. "What do you think?"

Daphne wrinkled her nose, but she was grinning. "It's... wow. It's beautiful. And just look at the waves crashing!"

Hope smoothed her hand over the girl's hair and pulled her in close for a one-armed hug.

"We're going to have lots of fun here this summer, huh?" Daphne asked.

"Yes, we are. Just like Uncle Christian and Gideon and I did. We used to get into so much trouble!" She tugged on the girl's hand and led her to the French doors at the back of the house that opened into the dining room. "Let's open some windows, and then we'll head into town and go grocery shopping and see what else we can find."

"Aren't we going to bring our stuff in first?"

Hope laughed softly and shook her head. She rummaged through her purse until she found the tiny abalone shell keychain with the keys to the cottage.

The cottage was furnished with a haphazard collection of furniture her family had brought out over the years, and not one piece was newer than twenty years. Somehow, the randomness of it suited the place as much as the nautical knickknacks scattered everywhere. Except for the den, which jutted out the back, the cottage was a simple rectangle. The dining room, kitchen, and bathroom occupied the southern side, and the den, stairs, and living room took up the north. It was on the small side, but open and inviting with its white walls, scarred cedar floors, and exposed, dark-stained beams. A big stone hearth stood proud in the middle of the northern wall in the living room, and Hope almost sighed with contentment as memories of rainy nights spent in front of a crackling fire paraded through her mind.

The air inside the cottage was musty and stale, but after she pushed the thick drapes back from the numerous large windows, light streamed inside and the place *felt* open and airy even if it would be a few hours before it smelled like it.

Daphne followed her inside, wrinkling her nose again.

"Yeah, I know it stinks in here," Hope said, "but a little fresh air will clear it right out. Why don't you open those windows over there while I get these?"

Within five minutes, they had every window in the living area open, and a fresh sea breeze wafted through them, chasing out the dank air. Hope stepped into the kitchen and opened the refrigerator, praying her brother hadn't left any food in it to rot when he'd been here earlier in the year. There was nothing in it but a box of baking soda. Good.

They headed upstairs to open the windows up there, too. The upper floor covered only two-thirds of the main floor and was comprised of two small bedrooms and a sitting room with more picture windows looking out over the cove and the ocean beyond. Hope folded her arms on one of the window sills while her daughter investigated her room.

After a few moments, she pushed off the sill and headed back downstairs. She located the old notepad in its home beside the refrigerator and took it to the table. Digging a pen out of her purse, she made a list of things she needed to pick up in town. Once she was finished, she checked it twice, tapping her pen against her chin. She was forgetting something. Lifting her eyes from the notepad, her gaze drifted again to the windows. And then she remembered. She added the items to the list, beaming. Daphne was going to love *that*.

"All right, Daph, let's go!" she called up the stairs.

A clatter of rapid footfalls marked her daughter's descent. Hope shook her head, amused. For being such a small, light nymph, her little girl could make enough noise to make the breakers crashing against the rocky cliffs jealous.

Daphne joined her at the table, folding her small arms around her mother and resting her chin on Hope's shoulder while she peered at the list. She pointed to a word.

"What's that say?"

"Sound it out."

"Cand...less? Oh, candles!" She frowned. "What do we need candles for?"

"Other than for power outages—which happen a lot here...." Hope craned her head around and kissed her daughter's cheek. "You'll just have to wait until to-night to see."

"Can we get some clam chowder for lunch, Mom?"

"You betcha." Hope rose to her feet, tucked her shopping list in her purse, and offered her daughter a mischievous wink. "Race you out to the car!"

With squeals of laughter trailing after them, they sped out the French doors, across the deck and around to the driveway, which was barely long enough for her SUV to be safely off the narrow road that connected the houses on North Point. Daphne beat her to the car, and Hope slid in behind the wheel and turned the key in the ignition, laughing breathlessly.

"I love you, baby girl," she said.

"I love you, too, Mom."

Just after she turned right from North Point Loop onto the coastal highway, a building caught Hope's eye. It had a great view of the cove. The northern half, adorably called the Salty Dog Chowder House, promised exactly what she and her daughter were on the hunt for. The other half housed a shop called The Sea Glass Gallery, and a quick glance in the windows showed a lot of sea glass art—jewelry, wind chimes, and whatnot—and the usual touristy fair of kites, sand castle buckets, and nautical souvenirs. Like most of the buildings in Sea Glass Cove, the eatery and gallery were sided with cedar shakes. The trim around the doors and big picture windows sported a fresh coat of navy blue stain.

The chowder house was busy and she spied several people wandering through the gallery. Surprising for the middle of the week before the official start of tourist season and a little past the lunch rush. Food must be good.

There was no parking, but just as she was about to keep driving, a couple walked out of the restaurant and got into a car. She waited for them to pull out and snuck into their spot just as another car appeared around the bend in the highway.

The waitress, a beautiful woman a few years younger than Hope with sun-streaked medium brown hair and eyes the color of blue-green sea glass, led them to the only empty table in the place. Like her family's cottage, the Salty Dog had windows everywhere, and on a clear day like today with the sun far enough west to stream through them, the place was dazzling. Rainbows danced on the walls, cast by the sea glass and crystal prisms decorating the windows, and Daphne was unsurprisingly enthralled.

"Wow," the little girl breathed. "So beautiful."

Hope scanned the room but didn't expect to see any familiar faces. She hadn't ever spent enough time here to get to know anyone but a few of their closest neighbors, and several of them had sold their cottages and left Sea Glass Cove since she'd last been here. As she perused the faces, her gaze snagged on a man sitting at the counter near the door between the Salty Dog and the Sea Glass Gallery. At first, she thought she'd noticed him because their waitress had stopped to talk to him, but when her eyes remained defiantly on him after the waitress stepped away, she knew she would've noticed him regardless. She guessed he was about her age, and he was undeniably good looking with a sturdy, toned build, medium brown hair streaked by the sun and salty air, and that might be what had first captured her attention, but that wasn't what held it. There was an indefinable *something* about him, a sadness that haunted those sea-green eyes that tugged at her heart. The kind that came from a deep hurt dulled but not erased by time.

"Uh, Mom, you want clam chowder, too, right?"

Hope jerked her attention back to her daughter only to realize their waitress had returned to take their order. She hadn't even opened her menu yet. "I'm sorry. I was distracted by the, uh, wind chimes in the shop over there. They're gorgeous."

The waitress lifted a brow, and Hope's cheeks warmed. She was busted.

"His name is Owen," the waitress said. "If you want to know about the wind chimes, he's your man."

"He made them?"

"Yes, ma'am. Would you like me to call him over?"

"No, I don't want to interrupt his lunch. I can wait until we've all eaten. So, um, yes, I'd love a bowl of clam chowder."

"Would you like that in a sourdough bowl?"

"Oh, yes. That would be wonderful."

The waitress sauntered away, and Hope let out a long, contented sigh. Embarrassing though that might have been, she wasn't going to chide herself for either staring *or* getting caught. She was single, after all, and it was perfectly acceptable for her to appreciate a handsome man, right? Besides, it felt good to acknowledge that side of her again. It had been a long time since her baser instincts had been so unfettered by the stress of

making a living and trying to cobble her marriage together even as it poisoned her.

Relaxing back in her chair, she indulged in a guilt-
free, honest smile. It was good to be back in Sea Glass
Cove. She snuck another glance at the man. It was even
better to find a piece of herself she'd lost somewhere in
her fifteen years of marriage. Maybe she'd see about going on a date or two while she was here.

Two

"HEY, BIG BROTHER."

Owen eyed his sister with his spoon hovering millimeters from his mouth. She leaned beside him with her hip against the counter and a Cheshire cat gleam in her eyes. He sucked the spoonful of chowder into his mouth and savored it for a moment before he addressed her. "Is there a reason why you're interrupting my lunch again? I need to get back to work, Erin, and I'd really like to finish my chowder before I do."

"Whine, whine, whine. See that pretty woman at the table over by the window?"

"Which window?"

"Like you need to ask."

He didn't. He'd spotted the woman and her beautiful little girl when they'd walked through the door and again after he'd sensed her watching him. Svelte build and on the taller side, light brown hair pulled back in a short, playful ponytail, and blue eyes. And her daughter was the spitting image of her. "What about her?"

"She seems pretty interested in your wind chimes."

The way she said it with that devious smile hovering at the corners of her mouth told him the wind chimes were only part of the woman's interest, and not a large part.

"Don't even think about it."

"Come on, Owen. It's been three years."

"So?"

"So... Mom's getting antsy again."

"So... it's your turn to get married and give her a grandbaby."

"I'm not the marrying type."

Owen snorted. "How would you know? You've never given a man a chance to prove you might be."

"I have yet to date a man worthy of a chance."

Rolling his eyes, he ate another spoonful of his clam chowder. They'd had this conversation more times than he could recall, and for the last three years, it always ended the same, with him angry and bitter and heartbroken all over again, so he headed it off before his pleasant day took a turn south. He waved his hand in dismissal. "If that's all you wanted, buzz off."

"Just thought you might like to know you have an admirer. That's all."

She sauntered off to check on her tables, and Owen didn't watch her go. Fearing another interruption—this time from his mother, because Erin was sure to mention the woman and her daughter as soon as she returned to the kitchen—he ate the rest of his lunch in a rush and carried his dishes into the kitchen.

"Amazing as always, Mom," he said. "Thanks."

"You're done already?"

"I've got customers." A half-truth. He'd already checked with the couple browsing his gallery and they were waiting for the rest of their party to arrive for lunch. He leaned down, kissed her cheek, and scooted out of the kitchen just as his sister entered, suspecting closing time wasn't going to come fast enough today.

A few of the diners came into his gallery after finishing their lunches, and most bought something. When one woman—a young mother of twin girls who reminded him strongly of his wife—begged her husband for his most expensive wind chimes and two kites, he threw in a sea-glass pendant for each of their girls.

"You don't have to do that!" the mother said. "Please. Let us pay for the necklaces."

"Their smiles are payment enough," he replied. "Please. My gift."

"If you're sure…."

"I am."

"What do you say, girls?"

"Thank you!" they chorused.

"You're most welcome."

Sensing someone watching him, he turned toward the Salty Dog and found the woman his sister had mentioned standing in the doorway between the two businesses with a curious expression. When their gazes met, her cheeks pinkened prettily. What had his sister said to the poor woman?

He ambled over to her, extending his hand in greeting. "I'm Owen."

"Hope," she said, shaking his hand. "And this is my daughter, Daphne."

"Daphne St. Cloud," the little girl said. "Well, my name is actually Daphne Andrews, but since Mom and Dad aren't married anymore, I want to go by St. Cloud 'cause I like it better. It's special."

Owen's brows rose. Hope's embarrassment darkened into mortification.

A divorcée, huh? Curiosity sparked.

"It suits you," he replied to the girl.

"I'm sorry," Hope said in a rush. "She's not usually so chatty around strangers. In fact, she's usually so shy she hides behind me."

He studied her with narrowed eyes as she recovered from her shock. Up close, she was even prettier, and she glanced over him with an intriguing appreciation that made his pulse quicken.

It had been a while since he'd felt *that*.

Clearing his throat, he said, "Erin said you might be interested in some wind chimes."

"Erin? Oh, our waitress. Right. Yes, I was admiring your wind chimes. Did you find all the glass on the beach here?"

"Yes, ma'am, I did."

"There's glass on the beach?" Daphne asked, concerned.

"Lots of it," Owen replied. He snatched another necklace—this one braided twine woven with a half a dozen varied pieces of aqua and cobalt glass and as many bits of iridescent abalone shell—and squatted in front of the girl. "The ocean tumbles it against the sand and rocks and takes off the sharp edges. See how smooth and soft it is now?"

"Oh...."

He glanced at her mother. "May I?"

Her brows dipped briefly, and she opened her mouth to object.

"My gift," he interrupted. "It isn't the first one I've given away today, and it probably won't be the last."

"How do you make a living if you keep giving your products away?"

"The best things in life can't be bought." He offered a tight smile. "Take it from someone who knows too well how precious and how brief those things some-

times are. There's a mirror just ov⟨
you want to look."

The little girl trotted away, and ⟨
him. She snapped her mouth closed, and ⟨if
the cogs working in her mind as she unta⟨
statement, searching for what he meant by it.

"Besides," he said quickly before she could ask,
"this is probably the *very* least I can do to make up for
my sister."

"Your sister?"

"Erin. Your waitress. I don't know what she said
to you, but I'm sorry it upset you."

"It didn't," she said hastily. "She just caught me
off guard."

He nearly groaned. "Please tell me she didn't stick
her nose completely in it."

"In what?"

"For the last three years, her goal in life has become setting me up with a new woman."

Her gaze shifted to his left hand, and she
frowned. The indentation from his wedding ring was
still there; he'd stopped wearing it only a few weeks ago.

"You're divorced?" she asked.

"Widowed."

Sympathy rounded her eyes, and when she replied, her voice was distractingly soft. "I'm so sorry."

He nodded in acknowledgement.

Abruptly, she straightened. "Wow."

n?"

this is a dark and rather deep conversation for a y day between two strangers."

"So it is." Grateful for the proverbial open door through which he could escape the conversation, he walked through it with her. "How about those wind chimes?"

By the time she and her daughter left the shop with a brand new set of sea-glass wind chimes for their family's cottage—somehow he wasn't surprised she was one of the St. Clouds who owned the cottage on North Point Loop just one driveway over from his—he was struggling to keep the memories at bay. He glanced at the abalone shell displayed on the wall behind his cash register. It wasn't either of the two he'd found, but it brought them and the days he'd found them to mind.

Suddenly, spending the afternoon gathering more sea glass and shells for his projects sounded like a fan- tastic idea. He called his lone employee, who was only too glad for the extra hours. Within half an hour, he was parking his truck in front of his house on the point. He grabbed his scavenging sack and headed along the gravel path that connected his home, the cottage next to it, and Hope's to the stairs that led down to the tiny and aptly named Hidden Beach tucked away between two arms of the point. Compulsion drove him down the stairs and straight for the natural rock arch that, at low tide, pro- vided a direct path to the main, mile-long beach.

THE ABALONE SHELL

It was there in that tunnel of stone that he'd found the first whole, pristine abalone shell. Every other time he checked down here, he'd found only fragments of shells no larger than a couple inches across, and that's all he expected to find today.

He recognized the iridescent crescent sticking out of the course sand immediately and stooped to pick it up. It wasn't a whole shell, but it was almost half of one and among the largest pieces he'd ever found on the beach of Sea Glass Cove. He skimmed his fingers over its shimmery interior as he strolled under the arch to the main beach, ignoring the sea glass littering the shore, and glanced up at the St. Cloud cottage perched high above him.

The little girl Daphne was out on the deck—of course she was—and despite the distance, she spotted him. He returned her exuberant wave, absently turning and twisting the shell fragment in his hand. After three years without so much as a flicker of interest in a new woman, the immediate pull he felt toward Hope was as bright as the lighthouse's lantern on the blackest night. How long were she and her daughter going to be in town? And would it be long enough to investigate this undeniable attraction?

Three

"HE'S FINALLY COMING BACK."

"Who is, baby girl?"

"Owen. He's been out walking the beach a long time. What's he doing?"

"Probably looking for glass and shells."

"Ooooh, duh."

Hope shook her head in amusement. She finished chopping the celery and tossed it in the salad and then wiped her hands on the dishtowel before joining her daughter at the dining room window overlooking the main beach. Sure enough, there was Owen, picking his way slowly toward the arch. He was cutting it close. The tide, which had just barely retreated far enough for the tunnel to be passable when he'd gone out was now nearly high enough to block it again. And it was a long walk home along the road—about half a mile—if he missed the window of opportunity.

Realizing she was staring at him again, she spun away from the window and poured herself a glass of iced tea from the pitcher she'd brewed as soon as they'd gotten home from their excursion. She squeezed in a healthy puddle of honey from the local bee farmer, added a few drops of fresh lemon juice, and purred with the first sip. She wandered over to the window above the kitchen sink, and her gaze drifted down to the beach. Owen had disappeared from view, and disappointment dampened her enjoyment of her drink.

"Can we invite him to dinner, Mom?"

Ice tea sprayed all over the sink and the back-splash, and Hope mopped it up while she recovered from her shock. The memory of their first meeting and her embarrassment at the hands of the man's sister were still fresh in her mind. There was absolutely no way they could invite him to dinner after that. And yet, she couldn't bring herself to say no to her daughter.

"We just met him, baby girl."

"So? He's really nice."

Hope couldn't argue with that. "That may be, but we can't invite strangers to dinner simply because they're nice."

"Why not? Isn't that how you make friends?"

How was she supposed to answer that? Every excuse that came to mind—it was too soon after her divorce, Daphne's father wouldn't approve, and the sneaking suspicion that if she invited the attractive gallery owner to dinner it wouldn't end at simple friendship—were all too complicated and abstract for Daphne's innocent young mind to fully grasp.

Finally, she came up with a compromise. "He may not want to, sweetie."

"Can't we at least ask?"

"I suppose." Hope sighed, resigned. "It's the neighborly thing to do, and since we're going to be out here all summer, it might be nice to have some friends. You're right, my darling."

Beaming, her daughter continued to stare out the window, waiting for Owen to crest the stairs from Hidden Beach. Hope couldn't deny that she was curious to see if the man would accept their invitation and more than a little hopeful that he would.

"There he is!" Daphne cheered and zipped out the French doors.

Hope followed her out onto the deck, equally amused and dismayed by her daughter's giddiness. The girl bounced with excitement as she waited for Owen to reach the main trail that connected the houses of North Point Loop to the stairs.

"Owen!" Daphne called, waving exuberantly.

He didn't hesitate even a beat before he turned toward their cottage as if that had been his intended destination even before Daphne's greeting. His long strides eroded the distance between them with remarkable speed, and Hope watched him, entranced. He had to be a couple inches over six feet, and the power and grace in every movement of his body had her pulse humming.

When he reached the bottom steps, he grinned, and Hope's heart tripped over itself.

"Hiya, Daphne St. Cloud," he greeted the girl. "I found something on the beach you might like."

He reached into the canvas sack hanging from his shoulder and pulled out a large fragment of abalone shell. Daphne's eyes lit up, and she glanced at Hope, asking permission to take a look at it. Hope nodded.

"What is it?" the girl asked.

"It's an abalone shell," he replied. "Well, part of one."

"It's beautiful. It looks like the shells on my necklace."

"That's because the shells on your necklace are abalone. There are tons of small pieces like those all over the beach, but one like this is a lot harder to find."

"Are there any whole ones?"

"Sometimes, but they're incredibly rare."

"How come?"

"They usually break against the rocks when the waves carry them to the beach."

"Have you ever found a whole one?"

"Just two."

"I want to find one. That'd be so cool."

Owen laughed indulgently. "I hope you do."

He raised his gaze to Hope, and his smile was slightly warmer than she would've expected from a man she'd met only hours ago. It did funny things to her heartbeat, and the husky tenderness in his voice when he spoke made her quiver deep inside.

"Hello again, Hope. Lovely evening, isn't it?"

Unable to tear her eyes from his sea-green ones, she nodded. "Beautiful."

She wasn't referring entirely to what was indeed a stunning evening, and there was a gleam in his eyes that told her he was aware of her double meaning. Suddenly realizing he was still standing at the bottom of the steps, she invited him up to the deck.

Swallowing the sudden and unexpected flare of desire, she put on the most gracious and welcoming smile she could manage. "Daphne would like to invite you to join us for dinner."

"Oh, yeah!" the girl piped. "Sorry. I forgot to ask. Will you come for dinner, Owen? Please?"

Lord almighty, he was sexy, and his physical attributes weren't half of his appeal. The way he focused on her daughter when he spoke with her was such a stark contrast to her ex-husband's detached parenting style that it left her a little breathless and dizzy.

"That's very kind of you, sweet pea," he said, "but

I don't want to impose on you and your mom."

Somewhere in the back of her mind, Hope wondered if she should've taken the easy out he offered, but before she could stop herself, she said, "It's no imposition. I still haven't mastered the art of cooking for one less, so we have plenty of food. It's nothing fancy. Just spaghetti, garlic bread, and salad."

"If you're sure you wouldn't mind, that sounds a lot better than the leftovers I was planning to reheat for myself."

"And maybe after you can help us with the candles," Daphne said. "Mom bought a bunch at the supermarket today, but she won't tell me what we're going to do with them. She just says I have to wait until tonight."

Hope frowned at her daughter, folding her arms across her chest and giving her daughter her best mom glare. "Daph, you're being a pest."

The little girl ducked her head. "Sorry."

"She's fine, Hope," Owen said with a gentle smile that disarmed her. "Honestly. I don't mind."

"Well, all right. Come on in."

Daphne raced into the house ahead of them still gripping the broken abalone shell. Hope and Owen followed at a more sedate pace, and she was surprised when he joined her in the kitchen and asked how he could help. He might've asked merely to be polite, but he said it so automatically that she doubted it.

"As my mom always says, the first time you eat over, you're a guest. After that you're family."

"Are you planning on having me over more than once?" he asked.

Oh, he was quick. Blush warmed her cheeks, and she lowered her gaze. "Maybe. We *are* neighbors, after all. Is that a problem?"

"Not at all. But, since we're neighbors, I think we can do away with the formality. So, how can I help?"

"There's not much else to do. The noodles are cooking, the sauce is done and simmering, the bread is in the oven, and the salad is tossed. Besides, it would be rude of me to invite you over and then put you to work."

"Psssh. It feels ruder of me to not help. It's weird sitting back and watching someone else cook."

"Did you do all the cooking…." She started to say *when your wife was alive*, but stopped herself in time and let her question hang as it was.

"No, Sam and I used to have so much fun cooking together."

"Sam? Your wife?"

He nodded. "Samantha." He shifted his gaze out the window and his expression turned softer, poignant. "We spent so many nights just like this in the kitchen together. I loved it."

"So many but not nearly enough," she surmised.

"No, not nearly enough."

She couldn't imagine Dan ever making such a statement, let alone with such genuine fondness and longing. As soon as the thought entered her mind, she shoved it right back out. She was done thinking like that, and she had promised herself she wouldn't compare her ex to the man or men she dated after him. She'd needed to end her marriage to him for the sake of her sanity, not because he was a bad man. She would not be one of *those* ex-wives, the kind fixated on destroying the men who wronged them.

Suddenly, Owen turned his attention back to her and smiled brightly. "All right, since there isn't anything for me to help you with here, it's only fair if I have you and Daphne over for dinner sometime."

Habitually, Hope said, "We couldn't impose." She started to say something else, but the look he leveled at her—brows lifted, eyes narrowed, and the corners of his mouth turned up in amusement—silenced her. Laughing, she held up her hands. "We'd love to. Thank you. And actually, I do have something for you to do."

She pulled out plates and silverware and handed them to him. As he took them, something stirred in the back of her mind. *Three* settings... and not because she'd once again fallen prey to habit. Sensing his eyes on her, she looked up to find him watching her with a faint, understanding smile. He turned away and asked Daphne if she would please give him a hand. The girl eagerly complied.

Hope frowned. What was she doing? She'd barely been divorced six months. She shouldn't be contemplating things like adding that third setting back to her table, and she *certainly* shouldn't be fantasizing about a man who was little more than a stranger… no matter how attractive and considerate he was. She'd just freed herself from one burden, and there was no way she was going to saddle herself with another any time soon.

Owen returned to the kitchen, and she could only stare dumbfounded as he slipped the garlic bread out of the oven, grabbed a bread knife from the block on the counter, and sliced it. As if he'd cooked a hundred meals in this kitchen. As if he belonged in it. She was still staring with her mouth hanging open when he carried the bread and salad to the table.

"I don't know how you prefer to serve the spaghetti," he said from the dining room. "Sam and I always just mixed the noodles and sauce together."

"Uh… yeah," she said slowly. "That's how we do it, too."

Hope shook herself out of her stupor and finished the spaghetti with a sly smile, determined to put away her doubts and appreciate a man who seemed to enjoy her company as much as she enjoyed his. Besides, a man who still missed the little pleasures like cooking dinner with his wife wasn't the kind that would ever be a burden.

Four

THEY REMAINED AT THE TABLE long after they'd finished eating, listening to Daphne chatter about the million things that fascinated kids her age, and Owen's
heart was lighter and freer than it had been in too long.
He loved his mother and sister dearly, and he was grateful they'd gone out of their way to try to fill the void in
him, but it wasn't the same. Dinner was delicious—
probably more so because of the charming company—
and the resulting languor settled over him. He leaned
back in his chair with his hands knitted behind his head
and his legs stretched out in front of him, utterly content.

"She'll go on all night unless we stop her," Hope
murmured as her daughter regaled them with a lengthy

description about the baby goats their neighbor in Montana had asked her to help bottle feed earlier in the spring. "Especially about Pam's farm. I swear, she talks about it in her sleep, too."

"Let her talk. I'm enjoying it."

Hope lifted a brow, and a moment later, she frowned.

"What?" he asked.

Her quizzical expression was adorable, and it was all he could do not to smile in response, but he tried because he didn't think she'd appreciate him jesting when she was being serious.

"You love kids."

"What's not to love?"

"I don't know," she replied slowly. "It's just that I haven't met many men as patient and natural at dealing with kids as you are."

"I've had a lot of practice." He shrugged and glanced out the window. The sun drifted near the horizon. "If you want to get your candles set up before nightfall, we might want to get dinner cleared and the dishes done."

"You're going to stay for that?"

"Daphne invited me, and as long as you don't mind, I'd love to."

Owen rose to help clear the table and she flashed him an uncertain smile. With that and the way she'd reacted earlier when he'd taken the bread out of the oven, he was beginning to suspect she and her ex-husband hadn't shared the household chores like he and Sam had. Was that part of the reason their marriage had ended? She seemed like a strong and independent woman, and she was clearly capable and comfortable with caring for her daughter on her own. It was easy to see her as the breadwinner of her family, and if she was, it wasn't hard to imagine her being frustrated with a spouse who didn't pick up the slack on the household side of things.

He filled the sink with hot water and squirted dish soap into it while she told her daughter to bring out all the candles they'd bought and the boxes from the closet under the stairs marked "lanterns". He scraped the plates she brought in into the trash and sunk them into the water. She positioned herself next to him with a dishtowel over her shoulder, and seamlessly they worked as a team with him washing and her rinsing and setting the dishes in the drainer on the counter beside the sink.

"I don't think in all that talk at dinner I heard what you do for a living," he said.

"I'm a writer."

He glanced at her, tugging the dishtowel from her shoulder to dry the dishes. He didn't know where they all went, so he figured he could dry them and let her put them away. "It's pretty rare to make enough to live off, isn't it?"

She nodded. "It can be. And sometimes it's as

much luck as hard work, but with self-publishing, writers have a bit more control over their destinies."

"Do you self-publish?"

"Some. I'm what they call a hybrid author. I started with a traditional publisher, and I still have a couple series with them, but the rest I self-publish. It wasn't until I took the indie path that I started making enough to pay all the bills, and it's been an amazing journey. I like having control over my career."

"What do you write?"

"Romance." She snorted. "With the divorce, I feel like a bit of a fraud. Silly, I know, but it's made writing a bit difficult."

"It may be silly," he replied, handing her the last plate, "but it makes sense given the genre you write. Is that why you came back to Sea Glass Cove?"

Again, she nodded. "I needed to get away from all the memories for a while. Recharge. And I haven't been out since before Daph was born."

"Really? Why?"

"We live in Montana, so getting out here isn't easy, and my brother or cousin were usually hogging it on the few occasions we might've had a chance to come out."

"I bet Daphne was disappointed."

"Oh boy. She's been begging me to bring her out for a long time… so, I figured this summer was a perfect time to do it. Poor kid's never seen the ocean. And she still hasn't been down to the beach."

"We'll have to rectify that tomorrow."

"That's the plan... and since *you* mentioned it first—" She laughed, and he soaked it up. It was such a warm, rich sound. "—it'd be fun if you joined us."

Even if he'd wanted to, he couldn't say no to her. "I'd love to."

After the dishes were stowed, and she'd wiped down the table, counters, and stove, she turned to him. "What about you? What brought you to Sea Glass Cove?"

"My parents' divorce. I was ten. Erin was six. Mom found this cute little run-down restaurant and decided that would be her life's purpose from that point on."

"That was the Salty Dog?"

"Yep. The rest, as they say, is history. She's done well with it."

"I can see why. Lunch was delicious." Hope lowered her gaze, chewing on her bottom lip. "Was it hard on you? The divorce?"

"It took some adjusting, sure. But honestly, it was the best thing that could've happened. For all of us." He narrowed his eyes and studied her expression. Guilt etched lines into her face, and he wished he could tell her everything would be all right and that she and her daughter would adjust like he and his sister and mother had, that the divorce might be for the best. But he didn't know why she'd left her husband, so all he could do was offer her an explanation of his situation and let her decide if it was helpful or not. "My father was an alcoholic, and he liked to push my mother around."

"Do you have any contact with him?"

"Nope. Haven't talked to him since the court granted Mom full custody. The night she left him, he knocked her down, and I hauled off and punched him. Broke his nose, blackened both eyes. I think that scared her more than anything—that I might become like him."

Hope tilted her head and scrutinized him with narrowed eyes just like he'd done with her a moment ago, peering deep into his soul with that intent gaze. "I don't think you have that kind of meanness in you. You're too kind to kids."

"Maybe you're right, but even the kindest hearts can be twisted and tortured into breaking." He stuffed his hands in his pockets. "Anyhow, I'm grateful Mom was strong enough not only to get out but to raise us on her own. I don't like to think how we might've turned out if she'd stayed."

"She never remarried?"

"No. Didn't really date much until Erin and I were both grown. She's got a beau now who adores her, and she feels the same about him."

A tender smile softened her face. "I'd love to meet her. She seems like my kind of woman."

Recalling his conversation with his sister, he was certain his mother would love to meet Hope, too, and he wasn't sure he was ready for the incessant pestering that was sure to follow. Maybe this technically wasn't a date, but it was the closest thing he'd had to one since Sam's death. "I think you and she would get along great. A little too great, I think, once she finds out I had dinner at your place tonight."

"Wait." Disbelief splashed across her pretty face. "You can't tell me…. You haven't been on a date since your wife…?"

"Not a single one." He held his left hand out in front of him. "I only took my ring off a few weeks ago."

Her eyes rounded.

"Guess that means there's something special about you and your little girl," he said lightly. He meant it, but he was beginning to feel a little raw and he didn't want old heartaches to darken what had been a refreshingly pleasant evening, so he changed the subject. "So, how about those candles?"

Taking the hint, Hope joined her daughter in the dining room and helped her unpack the candle holders and lanterns. Owen stepped in to help, his nose tingling with the musty scent emanating from the boxes. It reminded him of those first weeks after he and Sam had bought their house—it had taken a while longer to clear out the stink because they'd moved in in the middle of winter and opening the windows hadn't been an option.

"I keep thinking it's strange we've never met," he remarked, "but I guess you haven't been out since Sam and I bought our house. We've only had it seven years."

"And it's been over eight since I've been out. You might've met my brother Christian or our cousin Gideon."

"I *have* met them. Gideon's little boy Liam made quite an impression around here."

She smiled fondly. "He's an adorable little devil."

"Yes, he is. He and Sean went down to Hidden Beach by themselves. Scared us half to death."

"Oh, Gideon told me about that! He was furious!" She laughed. Wagging a finger at her daughter, she said, "Don't you dare even *think* about going to the beach without me, young lady."

"I won't, Mom," Daphne replied. "So… what are we going to do with these?"

"Well, these ones here we're going to set in the windows." She held up an aqua mosaic votive cup. "The lanterns we're going to take outside and set all around the front deck on the railing, and then, when the sun goes down, we're going to light them all."

"Oh!" Daphne's face lit up brighter than a thousand candles. "That'll be so pretty!"

"I know," Hope said. "And there are a *lot* to put out, so let's get to it."

Owen grabbed a dozen of the votive holders and carried them for Hope. Daphne followed along behind them, setting candles in the holders as her mother set them out. He remembered Gideon saying something about the tradition but he couldn't recall exactly how the man had phrased it, so he asked Hope.

"Grampy started it the night my dad was born. A storm had knocked out the power, so he lit every candle and lantern in the house. He joked that this cottage glowed as bright as the lighthouse that night. Now, whenever a St. Cloud comes home to the cottage, we light the candles so—as he said it—Sea Glass Cove will have a second light house for a night."

Owen hadn't ever seen it, and while there was no way a few dozen candles could come close to the powerful beam of the Stalwart Island Lighthouse, he imagined it would be a breathtaking sight nonetheless.

"It's a wonderful tradition," he said.

She beamed at him like he'd made the perfect response. "I've always loved it. Dan thought it was dorky, and so does Christian's wife, so he doesn't do it anymore."

"I take it you don't like her much."

"She's all right, I guess." Hope snorted. "Okay, no, I don't particularly like her."

"She's a snob," Daphne remarked.

"Daph!" Hope covered her face, trying hard not to laugh. "That's not a nice thing to say."

"But it's true!"

"Maybe so, but sometimes we need to keep true

things to ourselves when they might hurt someone else. Right?"

Daphne nodded, too excited about their task to be bothered by the scolding. Owen chuckled.

"You've got a wonderful little girl, Hope."

"She's pretty special. I think I'll keep her," she said with amusement still thick in her voice. "Okay, at the risk of sounding like a country song, I don't know your last name."

"McKinney," he replied with a chuckle. He glanced at Daphne and smiled. "Maybe it's not as cool as St. Cloud, but I adore the woman who gave it to me."

"The woman? McKinney is your mother's name?"

He nodded. "She legally changed our last name to her maiden name after the divorce. Said she didn't want us to have anything linking us to that man."

"What was it before the divorce?"

"King."

"Mmm, yeah. McKinney's better. More unique."

"I agree." He set his last candle in the final empty holder and glanced back at the others. "I think that's all of them, and the sun's nearly down now. Can we start lighting them?"

All that remained of the sun was a sliver of burning orange wavering above the ocean, and it painted the sea stacks and rocky points and islands and beaches and the dark forests inland with a dim ruddy light.

"You take the left, I'll take the right?" Hope

asked.

She held up a pair of lighters he hadn't seen her grab. He took the one she held out to him and started from the left side of the deck steps, lighting candles as he went. With two of them, it didn't take long to light the three dozen candles and lanterns, but even so, the sun was long gone by the time they finished. They left the lighters on the dining room table, and joined Daphne on the deck to admire their handiwork.

It was magical. Corny though the term might be, it was the only one that adequately described the flames dancing all around them on the soft sea breeze and the wisps of crimson cirrus clouds above alight with the last rays of the sunken sun.

"Wow," Daphne breathed.

"Wow is right," Owen said, echoing her wonderment. "How could anyone think this was dorky? It's stunning. Sam and Sean would've loved it."

"All right, that's the second time you've mentioned this Sean," Hope said, turning to face him. "Who is he, and why do you say he *would've* loved it?"

Owen sighed, mourning the loss of that fleeting moment of pure amazement. There was no salvaging it now, not with the old ache returning to his chest, wrapping tightly around his heart. So he didn't disturb Daphne's enjoyment, he spoke quietly. "He was my son. And he was in the car with my wife when it went over the cliff."

Five

BY NOON THE NEXT DAY, Hope hadn't yet recovered from her shock. She could not fathom the pain of losing her child, but her imagination had woken her in the middle of the night with a terrifying dream about her daughter and ex-husband crashing through the guardrail and plunging over the edge of a coastal cliff into darkness. After that, she'd spent much of the night alternately lying awake and standing in the door of her daughter's room.

She hadn't known what to say to Owen after that revelation, and he hadn't offered any details other than to say his little boy had been only four and loved the beach. She had no idea how she was going to face him today, and her time for figuring that out was dwindling to seconds. He was due to arrive any moment.

His name coming from her daughter caught her attention, and she glanced sharply at Daphne. The girl was on the phone with her father. She'd tried to call him last night after the last candles had burned or blown out, but he hadn't answered. And of course he'd called back just minutes before Owen was supposed to show up. Typical. He had an uncanny ability to sense things that made her happy and a penchant for disrupting them. She listened to her daughter detail their evening last night and wondered how her ex was taking it. Daphne's side of the conversation didn't reveal much of his reaction; she was too busy doing all the talking. And to hear her tell it, Owen was amazing. From what he'd shown them so far, Hope was inclined to agree. Dan wasn't likely to appreciate that.

A knock sounded on the French doors, and despite the persisting shock over Owen's announcement and her daughter mentioning him to her father, Hope smiled and trotted to answer it.

Owen stood on the deck and the same canvas sack he'd had yesterday was slung over his shoulder, but this time it bulged with the unmistakable shapes of buckets and tiny plastic shovels. Her smile widened into a grin. Sand castles. She hadn't even thought about making them with Daphne today on the beach.

"Hi," she said breathlessly.

"Hi to you, too," he replied.

Suddenly, her worry over how she would face him seemed ridiculous. The knowledge that he had lost not only his wife but his son too changed nothing. He was still the same fascinating man who'd captured her attention so firmly from their first meeting. The only difference was that she now knew the exact reason for the sadness that often shadowed his eyes.

"Come on in," she added, stepping back to give him room to enter. "We're going to be a few more minutes. Daph's on the phone with her dad."

"Ah. I can wait outside."

"Why?"

"I don't want to make things awkward for you."

"Believe me, if anyone is going to make things awkward, it will be Dan."

"Mom!" Daphne called, almost on cue. "Dad wants to talk to you."

Of course he does. Hope joined her daughter in the living room and took her cell phone back from her daughter. "Hi."

"Thanks for making Daph call me last night."

"I didn't make her. She loves you, Dan."

"And I love her. I'm sorry I missed her call, but I worked late, and when I got home it was too late to call her back."

She almost asked him if he was still at the same job, but she stopped herself just in time. She wasn't supposed to care anymore. "It's all right."

48

"Sounds like she's loving it out there."

"It's a special place."

Dan hesitated, and she knew exactly what he was going to ask before the words came out of his mouth.

"Who's Owen?"

"Our neighbor. Well, he lives a house over, but close enough."

"And you invited him to dinner even though you just met him?"

Bristling, she said, "He's a friend of Gideon's." It was a stretch, but since their boys had played together a few years back—probably only weeks or days before Owen's son had died—that was close enough to the truth, too. Before Dan could quiz her on something that really wasn't any of his business, she said, "I don't mean to be short, but the tide's on its way out, and Daph and I are heading down to the beach."

"Just you and Daph?"

Her brows furrowed, but when she glanced at her companion, her lips curved. Screw it. "Owen might join us, too."

She expected him to question her judgment again, but he didn't.

"I thought I might try to make it out there in a month or so to visit my daughter."

"She'd love that."

"Would it be... too difficult if I stayed with you? I'd sleep on the couch or on the floor in the living

49

room."

Where else did he think he would sleep? In bed with her? Never again. Hope pressed her lips together and pinched her eyes closed. "I'm sorry, Dan, but yes, it would be too difficult, and really, you'll want to have her all to yourself without me hovering around."

Silence met her from the other end of the line, and five then ten then fifteen seconds ticked by. Had the call been dropped? Or had he hung up?

Then he spoke again.

"I miss you."

"Dan…." She opened her eyes and sought Owen. He was currently showing Daphne the contents of his sack, and the delight on both their faces made it easier to tell her ex-husband what she needed to. "I will always care for you—deeply—but I can't let you drag me down anymore. I'm sorry. I wish I could've made it work. I do."

Dan sighed. "I wish I wasn't so screwed up."

"For your sake, I do, too. I have to go. Please let me know when you want to come out so I can make reservations for you at one of the inns in town."

"I will. Tell Daph I love her."

"I will," Hope said before he could add that he loved her, too. Part of his continuing professions of love and respect for her were manipulation, but she was certain he *did* love her. And if she was going to hold to her decision to save herself from being dragged under with him, she had to remember that love wasn't enough to overcome what had driven her to walk away.

She ended the call and stood in the living room for almost two minutes while she regained her composure. When she sauntered into the dining room, she was able to greet Owen and Daphne with genuine excitement.

"Daddy asked me to remind you he loves you," she told her daughter.

"Is he really gonna come out to visit me?"

"I guess we'll see. You ready to dip your toes in the sand, baby girl?"

"Yeah!"

"Then let's get this show on the road."

They headed out to her SUV, and without being asked, Daphne grabbed her booster seat out of the front seat and moved it to the back so Owen, with those long legs, could ride shotgun down to the northern beach access. Owen leaned back to help her untangle the seatbelt, and Hope marveled at the difference between him and her ex despite her promises not to compare them. Dan would've waited for her to help Daphne or told the girl she needed to figure it out herself. Many a time, such incidences had ended in Daphne crying and Hope angry with Dan for his inaction.

She paused before she slid in behind the wheel of her car, bracing her hands above the driver-side door as the old rabbit heart rate threatened and breathing suddenly became a struggle. She couldn't seem to draw air deep enough into her lungs to satisfy them. Arching her back, she inhaled as deeply as she could and blew it out with her lips pursed, staring at the cirrus clouds drifting lazily across the sky.

Finally, she got in her car and started the engine.

"Are you all right?" Owen asked so quietly she barely heard him.

She glanced at him as she backed out of the cottage's driveway. "I will be soon enough."

He frowned, clearly wanting to say something else, but he looked away. His concern was touching, and she was glad her daughter had asked to invite him to dinner last night. She had no hope of naming exactly what it was about him that so enchanted her, but he had the opposite effect on her that her ex-husband had. Where Dan elicited anxiety, Owen soothed it. She might think it was the losses he'd suffered, but Dan had known plenty of his own, and from the sounds of it, Owen had known at least a few of the abuses Dan had known as a child, too. So what was it that made him so different?

Those thoughts occupied her mind all the way down to the parking area, but for all her pondering, she couldn't answer the question. With the sun shining brightly and her daughter bouncing in place, she decided it didn't matter right now. Right now it was enough to enjoy a stunning day at the beach with her daughter and their charming neighbor.

The tide was retreating down the beach, and they decided to build sand castles first and hunt for shells and sea glass later. Because Owen was the more experienced sand castle builder, she let him take command, hunting down the objects he and Daphne asked her to find to add to their delightfully whimsical castle. After she'd collected enough to satisfy her daughter's artistic demands, Hope sat and curled her toes into the cool, damp sand.

When Daphne had mastered the technique for packing the sand in the buckets, Owen retreated to a driftwood log nearby with Hope and let the girl continue work on the castle by herself.

"Feeling better yet?" he asked softly enough that Daphne wouldn't be able to hear him over the surf.

"Not as much as I should be."

"I'm probably stepping far beyond my place, and I apologize for eavesdropping, but if a phone call was enough to make you so anxious, what's going to happen if he comes out here for a visit?"

She'd known him barely twenty-four hours and she'd kept her secrets and her hurts so close to her heart for so long that the part of her still beholden to old habits shied away from his inquiry. But she wanted to tell him. His quiet, unassuming nature invited her to trust him in a way Dan's mood swings and intensity never had.

"More of the same," she replied. "But we have a daughter together, and I'm going to have to learn how to hold my ground with him."

"What went wrong? If you don't mind me asking."

"I got tired of trying to be strong for all of us when he's determined to sabotage himself. I couldn't fix someone who wouldn't help fix himself, and it was destroying me."

The way he gazed at her with sympathy emanating from those kind green eyes….

A lump formed in her throat, and she tried to swallow it as her eyes tingled. She had to look away. She wanted to tell him how it hurt her to think she'd failed her husband and that she was struggling to admit that Dan's issues—and his inability to overcome them—weren't her burden to own, but the words stuck in her throat, tangled with the unshed tears.

He reached over and tucked a strand of her hair behind her ears. It was a simple, unconscious gesture that was anything but to her. He searched her face, and she found it odd that *she* was the one needing a shoulder to lean on. Lord almighty, the man had lost his wife and son. What was a divorce compared to that?

"How did losing them not break you?" she blurted.

He turned his gaze out over the ocean, and the muscle in his jaw worked. "It came close, believe me."

Eyes wide, she traced every line of his face. There were traces of grief, but they were faint, outshined by the fondness he had for his family. After a moment, he met her gaze again, and his features gentled.

"I'm not in danger of breaking into a million pieces anymore, Hope. I will always miss them, but I've reached a point that I can focus on the good times now without the grief overshadowing them. And when I reached it, that's when I was finally able to take my ring off and let them go."

"But—"

"There's no but. Nothing can bring them back, and forgetting that I'm still alive is a poor way to honor their memory, don't you think?"

She nodded. "How did you do it? How did you get to that point?"

"I had a strong support system here, namely two very strong-willed and big-hearted women. Something I suspect you haven't had through your divorce."

That was the truth. Her parents were in Washington, her brother was in California, her best friends were scattered all over Montana and Washington, and she and Dan had moved so many times since they'd graduated college that they hadn't had a chance to build the kind of lasting local friendships she could've relied on. And he'd inadvertently driven a wedge between her and the few she'd managed to find along the way.

She wrapped her hands around the back of her

neck and let out a growl of frustration. She had to stop thinking like this. It was ruining a beautiful day and her daughter's first experience with the beach and the ocean.

As she mulled over Owen's words and wondered how she could get herself to the point that she could look back on her marriage with detachment from the bad and appreciation for the good, a thought occurred to her. She dropped her arms and jerked her head toward him.

"Why us?" she asked.

"Why you what?"

"Last night you said you haven't been on a date or even to dinner with a woman … so why us? Why Daph and me?"

One corner of his mouth lifted in an adorable, lopsided grin. "Don't know yet. But you can bet I'm curious to find out."

The non-answer should've annoyed her, but it didn't. Instead, it made her laugh, and as amusement and what felt a lot like joy rippled through her, she decided she didn't care why. "So, we're going to wing it and see what happens?"

"Sounds like fun, doesn't it?"

"Yeah," she said, laughing a little more, "it does."

"And speaking of fun, it looks like your daughter has finished her masterpiece."

Masterpiece was exactly the right term for it.

Daphne had decorated her castle with the shells and glass and pebbles Hope had brought, and it was a beautiful mosaic of blues, greens, and whites. She'd also added a guarding wall and dug a moat. Hope commended her daughter's project, and together, the three of them raced down to the water's edge with buckets to fetch water for the moat. As that task devolved into an all-out splash fest, Hope felt the last dregs of the anxiety slip away. This was what life was supposed to be about—the simple pleasures.

"I don't know how involved you want to get in the community while you're here," Owen said when they'd worn themselves out and retreated to the higher beach, "but I'm hoping you might join me for the annual Fun Run. It's this Saturday and raises money for the schools."

"What's the entry fee?"

"Twenty-dollars, but I'll pay for us all. It's only fair, since I'm the one doing the inviting."

"Does that count as a date?"

"You bet."

"And today? And dinner last night? Do those count as dates, too?"

"Absolutely. And dinner at my place Friday night when I get back from Mendocino. Unless you don't want them to."

She grinned. "I do, actually. What's in Mendocino?"

"A cousin's art gallery. I need to take her some more of my sea glass creations to display and sell. I leave first thing in the morning tomorrow, and I won't get back until Friday afternoon."

"And you think you're going to be up for cooking after driving all that way?"

"Yep. So… we're on for Friday and Saturday?"

She beamed. "It's a date. Or two, rather."

Six

OWEN SETTLED HIS GROCERIES on the counter and went through the motions of putting them away. Deciding he could bring his overnight bag in from the truck later, he wandered into the living room and sank into his recliner. He tipped his head back and let his eyes drift closed.

He'd forgotten how long the twelve-hour drive down to Mendocino was. Even with the day off in between to rest and visit with his cousin, he was bone-tired. Why had he thought he'd have the energy to cook dinner for Hope and Daphne tonight?

As soon as he thought of calling them to reschedule, his dismissed the idea. He would find the energy. Somehow. Because he'd missed them both more than he could've imagined over the last three days. He'd missed them enough that his cousin, whom he saw only four or five times a year anymore, had noticed his distraction and asked if she'd get to meet the woman and her daughter who had snagged his attention. He hoped she would keep to her promise and not mention it to his mother and sister.

A knock sounded on his front door, and he opened one eye to check the clock on the wall behind the TV. It was five-thirty already? He pushed himself out of his recliner with a grunt and scrubbed his hands through his hair as he trudged to the door.

As soon as he opened it, joy seeped through him, bolstering him.

Without hesitation, Daphne wrapped her arms around his waist, and he bent over to return her hug. Straightening, however, took some effort, and her mother noticed.

Hope glanced over him with sympathy softening her expression. "No offense, but you look exhausted."

"I am, but that's okay. It's good to see you two again."

"If you want to reschedule, we'll understand."

"I don't. Come on in."

He closed the door behind them and followed them into the living room. He gave them a quick tour. Like Hope's family's cottage, his house was decorated artistically with nautical elements and graced with numerous windows and a stunning view of the cove and the ocean, but it was larger—three bedrooms upstairs instead of two, one full bath downstairs and another upstairs, and a kitchen that was easily twice the size and far more modern. That last feature was his favorite, and he liked that it seemed to be Hope's, too.

"I planned to have dinner going by the time you two came over," Owen said as he pulled out the ingredients for his mother's famous fish and chips, "but I only got home about thirty minutes ago. The drive took longer than I expected."

"You won't hear any complaints from me," Hope replied. She winked. "So long as you let me help."

"I'm tired enough that I was tempted to beg you to help. Daphne, would you like to watch a movie while your mom and I cook? If that's all right with your mom, of course."

"That's fine," Hope said.

"What do you want to watch?"

He led the girl into the living room and opened the cabinet under the TV.

"Oh! I haven't seen a lot of these." Daphne skimmed her fingers along the spines of the DVDs, Blu-rays, and VHS tapes. "Can I watch this one?"

"Finding Nemo? Sure."

With the little girl happily ensconced in his recliner watching the movie, he returned to the kitchen to find that Hope had already thin-sliced the potatoes and put the oil on the heat.

"I would've started the fish, but I don't know how your mom does it."

He started to show her, and when she took his hands and tugged his arms around her, he froze. What was she doing?

After a moment, she smiled shyly over her shoulder at him. "Is this okay?"

"Yeah," he replied slowly. "Just unexpected."

He trailed a finger along her jaw, mesmerized when her eyes slid closed and she leaned into him. His heart jumped and something that had been dormant for three years awakened. It was probably pushing the limits of their new relationship, but he lowered his head and pressed his lips to the curve of her neck. She tilted her head away, baring her neck and encouraging him, and he exhaled, brushing his cheek against her silky soft skin and eliciting a shiver from her.

"Your whiskers tickle," she murmured.

"Sorry. I didn't have time to shave before I left Mendocino this morning."

"That wasn't a complaint."

Threading his fingers with hers, he brought her hand to his mouth and kissed her knuckles. "It feels like a different lifetime the last time I did this."

"It was. It hasn't been as long for me as for you, but it still feels like that was a different life. A different me."

"Mmm."

Reluctantly, they released each other because dinner preparation demanded it. He'd made this meal—and the rest that made his mother's chowder house so popular—so many times in his life that it didn't take long to finish dinner. He tried not to think about how nice it was to have someone help him make it again, to remind him how much fun it could be to cook and how rarely he mustered the energy to do it for himself anymore. Hope took the place settings he gathered into the dining room, and he watched her.

She was sexy in a subtle, unconscious way—completely natural, beautiful not in a striking, in-your-face way but in a way that invited his gaze to linger and brought to mind visions of snuggling together in front of the fire on nights while storm-tossed waves pounded the cliffs. It was the same kind of beauty that had first drawn him to his wife, derived as much from a generous and adventurous heart as from any physical attribute.

At once, he decided that she was well named. She'd certainly awakened a hope in him from the moment of their first meeting in his store.

She turned and started back to the kitchen, pausing mid-step when she caught him staring. "Why are you looking at me like that?"

"Like what?"

"I don't know," she said uncertainly. "Like you're pondering the secret of life."

He chuckled. "Maybe I am."

She caught her bottom lip between her teeth, glancing at him and away like she had something she wanted to ask but was either too embarrassed or too nervous to put it into words.

"Just ask."

Her eyes rounded and then she laughed softly, waving him into the dining room. As soon as she turned toward the narrow strip of wall between the two big windows, he knew exactly what she wanted to ask.

"Is that Sam?"

He nodded, tilting his head to study the upper of the two photographs. By strange coincidence, Hope's cousin was the photographer. He'd flawlessly captured the moment; he and Sam looked so young and happy, smiling for the camera with their arms locked around each other in the exact spot where they'd found the abalone shell together. The rock arch and the sunlit ocean provided a stunning backdrop.

"How did you two meet?"

"An abalone shell—the first whole one I'd ever found." He leaned over to pluck the shell in question from the center of the dining room table where it had sat since they'd first moved in together back when he'd still lived in the Forest Haven Mobile Village, in the single-wide trailer that was now his sister's. "I was walking toward the main beach from the stairs and she was coming the opposite direction, and we spotted it at the same time. She had *just* moved to Sea Glass Cove and it was her first walk on the beach."

"What a sweet story!" Hope cooed. "What brought her to the cove?"

"A teaching job—elementary art."

Hope let her gaze meander around his home, and a faint smile of appreciation played across her features. "I thought the artistry of your house was your doing, but now I think it was as much hers as yours."

"Definitely. We clicked, right from that first moment." He slipped a finger around one of hers and tugged her hand toward him. "Much like you and I clicked in my store over wind chimes. And to answer the question I know is on your mind, yes, I still miss her and I always will… but I missed you, too, these last few days."

The shy, pleased glow that ignited her smile kindled a matching fire in his heart. There was something special at work here, and he reached for it with both hands, eagerly and without hesitation. He let his thumb glide along her jaw, he lowered his head, aching to kiss her but waiting for her to close the gap.

Wondrously, she did, and he smiled against her lips.

"I've been wanting to do that for a while," he whispered. "Probably since dinner at your place the other night."

"You should've said something because I've been

wanting to do it, too."

Grinning, he closed his eyes and rested his forehead against hers, brushing the backs of his fingers over her cheek. Good lord, she had such soft skin, and it was all he could do to keep his caresses to this. A little voice whispered slyly that she wouldn't mind, but movement in the living room caught his attention, and he shifted his gaze to see her daughter approaching. She sought what had drawn their attention and spotted the pictures on the wall.

"Is that your wife?"

"Mmm-hmm."

"She's so pretty."

"Yes, she was."

"And this is your son?" Daphne asked, joining them. She pointed to the picture below the one of him and Sam. It was one Sam had taken of him and Sean getting ready to kayak the Jewel River where it meandered lazily through the sand dunes before making its final twist across the beach into the sea.

"Yep, that's my boy Sean."

Somehow, it was a relief that Hope had already shared that with her.

"I wish I could've met him. Mom said he'd be about my age."

"I think you two would've been great friends."

He didn't know what he'd expected Daphne to do, but it stunned him when she threw her arms around his waist and buried her face against his stomach. There was such strength in those skinny arms. He wrapped his arms around her head and shoulders, clinging to the anchor she provided as a wave of unexpected grief washed over him.

"I'm so sad for you," she murmured, her words muffled by his shirt. "You must miss them so much."

He nodded and tightened his arms around her, clinging to the warmth and innocence in her embrace, craving what he'd lost that day and finding a glimmer of it in this beautiful young girl. How was it that her pure offer of sympathy hit so much harder than all the expressions of grief and condolences he'd endured? His eyes stung, and he pinched them closed.

"I miss them terribly."

After a moment, she loosened her hold and he released her, but it was almost a minute before he could unclench his jaw. He squatted in front of her gripping her shoulders, and when he met her gaze, the smile that curved his lips and lightened his heart was genuine.

"But you know what?" he asked.

"What?"

"You and your mom are helping."

"We are?"

He nodded. "So much more than I can say." He glanced up at her mother and smiled. "I have hope again."

"Hey! That's my mom's name!"

Laughing softly and with his eyes still locked with Hope's, he replied, "I know it is, sweet pea. Rather fitting, if you ask me."

Suddenly, she noticed the shell on the table, and awe washed across her face. "Oh… wow. Is this one of the shells you found?"

"It is. The first one."

"Where's the other one?"

"I don't display it." Before the insatiably curious little girl could ask why and open the lid on memories he preferred stayed locked away, he offered an explanation. "It's not as pretty, and it doesn't have a fun story like this one."

"Oh. Okay."

He let out a breath, thankful she was content with that answer.

Later, after dinner while Hope helped him with the dishes and Daphne finished her movie, he caught his date frowning on several occasions. At first, he ignored it but after the fifth time, he dropped the plate he was washing back into the soapy water and tilted his head to study her expression.

"What's on your mind?"

Again, her brows furrowed as she slipped deeper into thought. "Are you serious about a relationship with me? Even knowing the baggage that comes with it?"

"If you're talking about Daphne, she's hardly baggage. She's an amazingly sweet little girl, Hope, and she's an incredible bonus to dating you."

"Well, that's wonderful to hear," she said, ducking her gaze with a shy smile, "but I was referring to my ex-husband."

"What about him?"

"At some point, if we stay together long enough, you'll have to deal with him."

"So?"

"That's a lot of baggage."

"Do I look put off?"

She narrowed her eyes, and after a moment, she laughed. "No, you look rather full of yourself, like you think it'll be all sunshine and rainbows."

"Believe me, I've been alive long enough and lived through enough to know that life has plenty of storms and dark nights." He contemplated the uncertainty shadowing her smile. "It's been three years for me, and that's plenty long enough. But maybe it hasn't been long enough for you."

She inhaled deeply, held it, and then let it out slowly. "Not really. I have to be honest with you. I didn't expect to start dating so soon."

"That's not much of an answer." He reached for her and tenderly touched her cheek, but she didn't look at him. "Hope."

Meeting his gaze, she sighed.

"I don't want to push you into anything you're not ready for," he said. "If you aren't ready for this, that's fine. Just say so. I'll understand."

"That's not it. It's just…." Suddenly, she smiled. "Unexpected."

He laughed and took her by the chin. When she didn't resist, he pressed his lips lightly to hers. "So, does that mean we're moving in a direction and a speed you're comfortable with?"

"Considering the fact that *I* initiated the first gesture of intimacy, it'd be a tad hypocritical of me to say no, don't you think?"

"That doesn't answer my question."

She laughed again, softer. God, he loved that sound. He loved it even more when she threaded her arms around his neck and angled her body into his, leaning back in his arms to gaze adoringly at him.

"The answer to your question is yes. Maybe it's sooner than I expected, but it feels right, and I want to run with it."

Seven

"I CAN'T BELIEVE HOW MANY PEOPLE came out for this," Hope remarked as she strolled along the paved path through the dunes. One hand rested in the crook of Owen's elbow and the other gripped her daughter's hand. "This is amazing. It looks like the entire town is out here."

"Pretty close," Owen replied. "It's one of the biggest fundraisers for the schools."

The first leg of the Fun Run started at the northern beach access and traveled along the highway, which was currently lined on one side with cars and on the other with booths selling various refreshments. The second leg returned via the dunes walking path. Most people walked at a leisurely pace and a few jogged, but even with the varied paces and the large crowd, the foot traffic was all headed the same direction today, and there was little in the way of congestion or collisions.

Hope, Daphne, and Owen had jogged a bit early—it was the Fun *Run*, after all—but he was still recovering from his whirlwind trip to Mendocino, and the day was so exquisitely clear that they wanted to slow down and savor it.

The fine weather wasn't the only thing Hope was savoring. Memories of last night swirled deliciously through her mind, and she could still feel Owen's lips pressed to hers, the warmth and strength of his arms around her, and later, the weight of his head on her shoulder when he'd drifted off in the middle of watching the rest of Finding Nemo with Daphne. She'd forgotten how nice it was to watch a man sleep, to enjoy that quiet, uncomplicated closeness with him.

"Feeling a little more rested?" she asked, smiling up at him.

"Yeah. Sorry I fell asleep on you guys last night."

"You won't hear me complain." Grinning wider, she added, "You're pretty cute when you're asleep."

"Thanks," he replied with a chuckle. He leaned down and pressed a quick kiss to her cheek. "I'll make it up to you. I promise."

"You seem to be laboring under the impression that there's something to make up for, and I guess as long as you are, I should ask how you plan to make up for whatever it is you think you need to—"

The shock as much as the kiss itself cut off her words. Lord almighty, the man was fast, and he could *kiss*. She'd never been much of a kisser herself, but the way he did it—clasping her face and drawing her body against his in the middle of a stream of people like he couldn't get close enough to her and didn't care who was watching—took her breath away.

Then he pulled away and started walking again like nothing had happened. Well, not *totally* like nothing had happened. A smug grin lit up his entire countenance.

Blushing, Hope glanced down at her daughter. Daphne watched her with a strange light in her eyes— part curiosity, part surprise, and part something that looked a lot like joy.

"What?" Hope asked her.

"You're happy. Like... *really* happy."

"Of course I am." Hope grabbed her daughter around the waist and picked her up, settling her on her hip even though Daphne was now so big it was a struggle to do it. "It's a beautiful day, and I get to spend it with my most favorite girl in the whole wide world."

Daphne opened her mouth to contradict that, but instead she only frowned. Then she threw her arms around Hope's neck and squeezed. "I love you."

"I love you, too," Hope murmured, wondering what thought her daughter wrestled with but didn't have the words to articulate.

Suddenly, she realized Owen had stopped walking. Turning back to him, she saw him staring ahead with his mouth pressed into a flat line, so she followed his gaze, pondering his sour expression as she immediately recognized the waitress from the Salty Dog Chowder House—his sister, Erin. She stood with another, exquisitely beautiful woman with long, wavy silver hair. The older woman's facial features and build were so similar to Erin's that she had to be the siblings' mother. After a moment, Owen sighed and started forward again. Hope set Daphne on her feet, took her daughter's hand, and reached for Owen's. He twined his fingers with hers and flashed a smile at her.

"What was *that*?" Erin asked when they reached her and the other woman.

"What was what?" Owen replied evasively.

"That back there. That *kiss*!"

He raised his brows. "You know what it was, and yet you're asking me?"

Sensing his unease, Hope extended her hand to his sister. "I know we've met, but perhaps a more proper introduction is warranted. I'm Hope St. Cloud, and this is my daughter, Daphne."

"Erin McKinney," the younger woman replied. Glancing at her brother, she scowled. "And I'm this brute's sister, in case he neglected to mention it."

"He didn't."

"It's a pleasure to meet you, Hope and Daphne. I'm Andra," the older woman said, shaking Hope's hand as she offered it. "I am Owen and Erin's mother."

"It's wonderful to meet you, too," Hope remarked. "Beautiful name."

"Short for Alexandra," Owen said, still holding his sister's glare with one of his own. "But Alex or Lexi or anything along those lines are far too mainstream for the unique powerhouse that is my mother."

"So, are you going to explain yourself or what?" Erin demanded of him.

"I'm going to go with 'or what'."

"And I'm not going to let you. Three years, Owen, without so much as a single date. I'm sure you can imagine our shock at seeing you kiss a woman in the middle of the Fun Run with the whole town as an audience. When were you planning to tell us?"

"When I was ready."

"And when, exactly, were you going to be ready?"

Several seconds passed in silence between them. Erin stared down her brother with unyielding determination, and when Hope's gaze slid from her to Owen, she stepped back. His eyes were bright with pain, and though she'd seen it in his eyes before, it had never been so bare or so close to the surface. Andra reached over and gripped her son's shoulder, but the reassuring smile he offered her convinced no one that he was all right. It didn't reach his eyes, and it took him too much effort to force it.

"Please don't push it, Erin," he murmured, lowering his gaze at last.

"But I just want—"

"Erin," Andra interrupted. "Enough. When he's ready to let us in on the details, he will."

"We were planning to play on the beach after the fun run," Hope said. "Why don't you join us?"

"If it's all right with Owen," Andra said, waiting a beat to gauge her son's response, "that sounds like fun."

They finished the Fun Run and slipped away to a quiet section of beach. With so many people out and about today, it wasn't easy, but they claimed a stretch of soft, dry sand just below the line of driftwood that the tides and storms had pushed up against the dunes. Erin didn't seem entirely appeased and shot frequent hooded glances at her brother. Andra was far more cheerful than her daughter and plucked blades from the grasses that blanketed the sand dunes while Owen and Daphne went in search of shells. When they'd found enough for whatever Owen had in mind, mother and son showed Daphne how to make necklaces from the grass and shells.

Erin sat beside Hope on a log that had long ago been worn smooth by the sand and waves and silvered by the sun and storms. For a long while, they sat in silence, observing the impromptu art lesson.

"If you're in the market for the last piece to complete your picture-perfect family, you won't find many better than my brother," Erin remarked at last. She wasn't smiling—not quite—but fondness for her sibling radiated from her like the warmth of the late spring sun overhead. "The man was made to be a dad."

"I don't know what I'm in the market for," Hope replied. "Or if I'm even *in* the market."

She didn't say it out loud, but watching Owen play with Daphne made it impossible to keep her promise not to compare him to her ex-husband. Dan had never paid Daphne the kind of attention Owen did, and when he'd tried, it wasn't ever as natural. Dan just wasn't cut out to be a parent, and considering his childhood and his parents, she even understood why. Owen came from a broken home, too, but at least he'd had a strong mother to make sure he knew what it was to love and be loved. Dan had been bounced from one parent back to the other and treated like the burden he was to them. How could he possibly be expected to have the same paternal drive and instincts Owen did?

Before the seed of guilt could take root, she ripped it out. Maybe he didn't have the instinct, but Dan was an adult and fully capable of making the kinds of choices to make up for his lack of innate knowledge. If he couldn't look to his parents as examples of what to do, he could've looked to them as examples of what *not* to do. Instead, he'd done neither and chosen to not be a parent, leaving Hope to do everything for Daphne.

"You're definitely right about your brother," she remarked. "He's such a natural with kids, and to be honest, I think we're both happy right now to let things happen as they will. There's no pressure, and after my divorce, that's incredibly refreshing."

Erin dropped her gaze to the sand, and she traced patterns in it with a stick for almost a minute before she replied. "I know he told me not to push it, but I can't help it. I lost my brother when Sam and Sean died, and he's been getting better and better, but he's still not the same Owen he used to be."

"I'm not sure a person can ever be who they were before a loss like that. That doesn't mean they can't be an even better person than they were before. Wiser. More appreciative."

"You're right, of course. It was just so hard to watch him hurt like that, and every time I see that look in his eyes again… it makes my heart break for him all over again."

"I'm sure it does."

"I just want to see him happy again."

"Of course you do. He's your brother."

Hope watched Owen tie the grass-and-shell neck-lace around Daphne's neck right below the one he'd given her that she only took off when she was in the bath. Perhaps she should be concerned that her daughter was already so attached to a man who might be in her life for only a moment, but she couldn't bring herself to worry about it. She couldn't see how a little more love could be a bad thing. If this didn't work out, then yes, that would break Daphne's heart, but even heart-break had a purpose; it was a valuable lesson on self-reliance.

And anyhow, Hope trusted Owen.

No matter what happened, she believed with a powerful certainty that Owen would do everything he could to spare her daughter from the worst of the pain.

"Hey, Erin!" Owen called. "You wanna come help Mom show Daph how to weave a mat? You're bet-ter at it than I am."

"Sure." Erin pushed to her feet and stood on her toes to kiss her brother's cheek as they passed each oth-er. "All I'm gonna say is bring her around again, okay?"

Owen only nodded and sat where his sister had on the log. "Sorry to leave you alone with the wolf like that, but I couldn't sit and let her needle me. I know she means well, but sometimes, I just can't deal with it."

"Don't worry about it." Hope narrowed her eyes thoughtfully. "She loves you, you know."

"I know she does." Sighing, he leaned back, brac-ing his hands on the log behind them. "But I have a lot of guilt where she's concerned."

"Guilt? Over what?"

"She broke up with her boyfriend—the most se-rious relationship she's ever had—right before the acci-dent, and I wasn't there for her. All our lives, I've made sure she could count on me to be there for her, but when it really mattered—when she most needed me—I wasn't."

"Owen, you lost your wife and your son. What's a breakup compared to that? Even a divorce?" She rested her head on his shoulder and tucked her arm around his waist, offering whatever comfort she could. "I'm sure she understands."

He shook his head. "On a logical level, I'm sure she does, but the heart is rarely logical. And me not telling her about us probably feels like another betrayal."

Hope started to tell him that his sister was plenty old enough to get over it, but her mind snagged on a single word he'd said. He could've said "not telling her about *you*", but he hadn't. He'd said *us*.

Her marriage had ended officially just six short months ago, but it felt like it had been years since she'd been part of an *us*, and her heart did a funny little flip-flop—not the kind of flip-flop that brought a surge of panic like it had done so often over the last few years but rather the kind that kindled a warm glow deep in her chest.

"If that's the case," she said slowly, "maybe you should just tell her about us. What there is to tell."

He tucked her hair behind her ear and kissed the top of her head. "You're right. I wanted to keep you to myself a little while longer, but Erin is more important to me than my selfishness. So… would you be all right if I invite her and Mom to our summer solstice bonfire next Sunday?"

"Our what?" Then a memory popped into focus of the mile-long beach lit up by dozens and dozens of bonfires. "Oh!"

She remembered her father telling her the townsfolk of Sea Glass Cove gathered on the beach every solstice and equinox to celebrate the changing of the seasons and to reaffirm their sense of community, but she hadn't been to one of them since high school.

"They still do that here?"

"If anything, the solstices and equinoxes are probably bigger events now than they used to be. The word has spread, and we get a lot of people from out of town. Especially for the summer solstice. Are you all right with Mom and Erin joining us?"

"I guess that means I don't have a choice about going."

He ducked his head sheepishly. "I was hoping you'd want to."

"Maybe I was hoping to have you all to myself." Suddenly, she grinned. "I'd love that, and of course I want them to join us! They're your family, and they're a part of you."

Hope's heart raced when he took her face in his hands, and as he brushed his thumbs over her cheeks, anticipation mounted. When he finally brought his lips to hers, she sighed with relief, eliciting a chuckle from him.

"Oh, come on, Owen!" Erin called. "You can't tell me not to push it and then kiss her like that right in front of us!"

This time, his reaction was decidedly amused. He laughed and turned his head to his sister with his arm draped around Hope's shoulders. "I can and I will."

For good measure, he kissed her again, and Hope thought the mischief in his sea-green eyes might be the most adorable thing she'd ever seen.

Eight

OWEN TOSSED ANOTHER cedar log on the fire and watched the sparks explode and dance into the sky. The fragrant smoke curled around him, a welcome and relaxing scent that brought memories of dozens of other solstice fires. As the sun sank closer to the horizon, more bonfires sprang up across the beach and music drifted to him on the breeze, accompanied by the ceaseless rhythm of the ocean. The tide was high but turning, and Owen anticipated racing across the damp sand with his party over the coming hours. Nearby, his sister and mother helped Andra's beau, Red, prep their dinner—steaks, shrimp, potatoes, and corn to be cooked over the fire and accompanied by a fresh green salad.

Hope and Daphne hadn't arrived yet, and he

glanced over his shoulder toward the northern parking area. They'd planned to come together, but when he'd walked over to her house, she'd been on the phone and told him with a grin that she'd meet him down at the beach in a bit, so he'd walked down. He returned his gaze to the fire and poked at it with a long stick, trying his best to ignore the disappointment creeping up on him. Had she changed her mind and decided not to come?

A dog barked behind him, and he glanced toward it. A grin split his face.

Striding toward him were Hope, Daphne, a boy the same age as the girl, and a man leading an excited black Lab. Owen recognized the man immediately; even with dark hair and those dark Spanish eyes so different from Hope's light brown and vibrant blue, the familial resemblance between the cousins was unmistakable. The St. Cloud genes showed through in their frames and in the bone structure of their faces. Owen rose from the driftwood log he'd pulled over as a makeshift bench and started toward them.

"Look what the dog dragged home," Hope said, beaming. "Gideon, you remember Owen, right?"

"Sure do," her cousin replied, extending his hand to Owen. "Good to see you again, man."

"Likewise." Owen squatted and opened his arms to the little boy. "You have grown so much I barely recognize you, Liam! How are you, little man?"

"I'm good!" Liam replied, throwing his arms around Owen's neck. He pointed to the young black Lab quivering beside her master as he held a stick up to keep her attention. "This is Shadow, our new dog."

"She's beautiful."

"Have you met my cousin, Daphne?"

"I have. And I gotta say, I'm pretty fond of her."

"Yeah. She's pretty cool for a girl."

Daphne stuck her tongue out at her cousin.

"Not only for a girl. She's just pretty cool period." Laughing, Owen pushed his body straight and gestured to their fire. "We're all set up and ready to celebrate. Mom and Red and Erin are getting dinner ready to cook, so pull yourselves over some driftwood and kick back."

As Gideon and his son and Daphne picked their way across the soft sand and threw the stick for the Lab to fetch, Owen slipped one arm around Hope's waist and leaned over to press a kiss to her cheek. She turned her head at the last second, surprising him, and a small groan escaped him when their lips met.

"Been wanting to do that again all day," she murmured.

"Mmm. Me, too."

She tilted her head back to gaze up at him. "You don't mind that Gideon's here, do you? I thought he'd cancelled this trip, but he changed his mind at the last minute."

"Why would I mind? I like your cousin."

"It's not too hard seeing Liam? He and your boy used to play together...."

He took her by the chin and kissed her again. "It's all right, Hope, but thank you for being so considerate of me. Honestly, seeing Liam again brings a piece of Sean back."

He liked the way she curled herself around him, offering support even though he didn't need it. With his arm still around her shoulders and hers around his waist, they made their way to the fire together as if they couldn't stand to be separated even long enough to walk the short distance.

By the time they reached everyone else, his family had brought the dinner fixings over and were waiting for him to get the fire ready for cooking. He quickly made the introductions.

"Hope, that handsome devil with his arm around my mother is Everett Castle, owner of the Grand Dunes RV Resort. You can call him Red. And Mom, you've met Gideon, but I don't think Erin has. Gideon is Hope's cousin, and Erin is my sister."

Pleasantries were exchanged, and after, his sister wasted no time putting him to work.

"Waiting on you, master chef," she remarked.

Owen poked and nudged the logs into place, dragged over the four large rocks he'd selected before he'd started the fire and arranged them how he wanted them, and then set the metal grate on top of them. He regarded his sister with brows lifted and his hand held out expectantly. She started handing him the items to be cooked, beginning with the foil-wrapped potatoes and corn.

"You have a place to stay?" Owen asked Gideon.

"Yeah. I reserved a hotel room weeks ago—right after Hope decided to come out to the cottage for the summer. I figured I'd let her have the place to herself."

"*Let* me have it?" Hope asked, nibbling at her salad. "As I recall, I said I was taking the cottage for the summer and anyone who wanted to visit was welcome to sleep on the couch. That invitation is still open, by the way, but Daphne and I are keeping the bedrooms. You and Christian and Mom and Dad and Uncle Matt and Aunt Maria have spent a lot more time out here than I have, so it's my turn."

Gideon lifted his hands in a show of peace. "Did I not say I reserved the hotel room for Liam and me so you could have the place to yourself?"

"And do you not realize I'm teasing you?" Hope quipped.

"I guess not. Been a while since you've been in a teasing mood. It's good to have you back, cuz."

Conversation turned to the festivities currently underway across the beach as the tide inched its way out, and shortly thereafter, Daphne and Liam begged the adults to go play. Erin suggested building a driftwood fort, and that was met with unanimous approval from all members involved.

"You coming, Gideon?" Hope asked.

"Nah. I think I'll stay here and help Owen with dinner. Indulge in a little male bonding, if that's all right with you ladies and Red. But take the dog with you, would ya? I'm tired of watching the drool dripping from her jowls."

"Really?" Owen inquired. "You'd rather work than play?"

"You know I like watching you cook," Gideon said with a pronounced lisp, wiggling his brows. "You big sexy bastard."

Owen laughed. Not to be outdone, he replied, "Oh, honey, keep talking dirty to me like that."

"Lord almighty," Hope said with laughter thick in her voice. "You two are as bad as Gideon and Christian together. Come on girls and boys. Let's leave the cooks to it."

Still chuckling, Owen watched her saunter a few yards down the line of driftwood to where Erin had found a perfect spot for their fort. For a long time while he tended the fire and dinner, he and Gideon were content to quietly watch the women and kids play and build.

Suddenly, his companion elbowed him and grinned. "You and my cousin, huh?"

"Seems so."

"Good luck with that."

Owen lifted a brow and studied Hope's cousin, trying to decide if the man was being sarcastic, and if so, why. Did he not approve? Or did he think Hope was difficult to deal with? Owen snorted. It *definitely* wasn't the latter. He'd met few people in his life who were as easy to be with.

"Seriously," Gideon clarified. "After fifteen years of putting up with Dan, she deserves a good man."

Owen let out a soft huff of laughter that was as much relief as amusement. "Thanks for that. I mean it. We just met a couple weeks ago, so I have no idea how far this will go, but... I never thought I'd get *this* far again. And that says a lot to me about the potential between us."

Gideon nodded. Then he laughed. "Just remember. If you hurt her, Christian and I are honor bound to avenge her."

"Thanks for the warning, but hopefully it won't come to that. Hopefully...."

He snapped his mouth closed, shocked by the force of the thought.

Hopefully it'll last.

It came out of nowhere and left him reeling. Not because he wasn't ready for the kind of relationship that didn't end—he was, and his time with Hope had driven that home—but because he suddenly realized that, logistically, it might not work. She was here for the summer only. Her home, her life was in Montana. What was he going to do when she returned to it? Because, as he let his gaze wander down the beach to take in the multitude of bonfires and the hundreds of people gathered around them, he couldn't imagine leaving Sea Glass Cove. This was his home, where all his happiest memories had been made.

"Whoa. Why so serious all of a sudden?" Gideon asked, leaning away.

Owen smoothed his expression. "Thinking about things I shouldn't be worrying about tonight."

"Well, knock it off. And why don't you go have some fun with my cousin? I can finish cooking."

"To be honest, sometimes it's as much fun to watch her."

"Stop it, big boy. You're making me jealous!" Gideon teased, again with the lisp. This time he stroked a fingertip down Owen's arm. "You're just so romantic!"

"Maybe I spoke too soon. Hope!" Owen called. Laughter made his voice waver. "Come save me from your cousin!"

"Sorry, dude. Habit. This is how Christian and I cut loose when we're together, and sometimes I forget people outside my family might not appreciate it."

"Was I not playing along earlier? Don't worry about it, Gideon. It doesn't bother me in the least. I'm just not used to it." Chuckling, he flipped the steaks and the shrimp. "You forget that I'm surrounded by women all the time, and they don't goof around the same way."

"In my experience, being surrounded by women is *never* a bad thing. Unless Hannah is one of them."

"That explains why she isn't here. You're over for good, then?"

Gideon nodded.

"Mind if I ask what happened?"

"Same thing that finally pushed Hope to leave Dan. I got tired of doing it all."

"That the reason for the Will Turner vibe you've got going on these days?" Owen gestured to the crisp anchor goatee and shoulder-length hair pulled back in a neat, low ponytail that made him look a lot like Orlando Bloom's character in the Pirates of the Caribbean movies.

Gideon let out a snort of laughter. "It was Liam's idea—he's obsessed with those movies—but yeah, she hates it."

"She really pissed you off this time." Owen prodded the coals and added another log to the fire. "So… you have custody of Liam?"

"Not yet, but I'm working on it. We're co-parenting right now, but it's not working. She just isn't reliable."

"If there's any way I can help, please call." Owen glanced at Gideon, noted the man's downcast expression, and it was a sharp contrast to the mischievous gleam that had lit up his dark eyes only moments ago.

"It's been a few years, but I haven't forgotten which of you was the reliable parent."

"Thanks, man. I mean it. I may need all the help I can get." Then, the smile was back. "And I'll pretend it has nothing to do with the fact that you're dating my cousin and possibly trying to buy my support."

"That didn't even cross my mind. It's the right thing to do."

"Good lord, man, you really *are* the product of an estrogen ocean. No wonder you've had such good luck with women."

"If you say it's because I *am* one, I will fillet you like a flounder and throw you on the grill right next to the shrimp."

"Ouch. That's brutal. And slightly cannibalistic." Gideon held his hands up, chuckling. "Remind me to stay on your good side."

Their conversation shifted to other topics, and when the food was cooked, Owen called everyone over to eat. He wasn't tooting his own horn, but the meal was delicious—why did food cooked over a fire always taste better?—and the company was amazing. A relaxed, celebratory air had settled over the length of the beach, and it was infectious. After everyone had finished eating, Gideon fetched his guitar from Hope's SUV, and his playing further deepened everyone's carefree enjoyment.

As the sun sank below the waves and colored the

sky with vibrant, fiery hues, Owen realized he hadn't enjoyed a beach party this much since that last one he'd shared with Sam and Sean. Things like this were always so much better shared with loved ones, and while his mother's and sister's company, and Red's and his sons', had made the last three years of solstices and equinoxes enjoyable enough, there had been a hole in him… a hole Hope and her beautiful daughter filled.

They sat on the log beside him but not close enough for his liking, so he pulled them closer.

"Thank you for coming out with me for this," he murmured close to Hope's ear.

"I can't imagine enjoying this with anyone else," she replied just as softly, tilting her face up expectantly.

He obeyed, kissing her gently and briefly, aware of their audience. How could it be that they'd known each other such a short time? And how could it be so different and yet the same as when he and Sam had first gotten together? So new and yet so comfortably familiar?

As sunset faded into twilight and twilight passed into full night and the tide retreated until finally reaching its lowest point of the evening, Owen and Hope and their party alternately lazed around, chatted with passersby, threw sticks for Gideon's black Lab until the poor thing collapsed in the sand, and built sandcastles by firelight. Finally, as they ticked closer to midnight, the two kids burned up the last of their energy, and even though he wasn't in any hurry to call it a night, Owen suggested he and Hope and Gideon get Daphne and Liam home and to bed.

"But I'm not tired!" Daphne whined through a yawn.

"Me, either," Liam echoed. A moment later, he too yawned.

"Uh-huh. Why don't I believe either of you?" Hope asked.

Because neither his mother and Red nor Erin were ready to turn in yet and because he was too tired himself to walk home, he hitched a ride with Hope and Gideon, squished in the back seat with the kids. Within minutes of being strapped into their booster seats, both children were out cold. Shadow, the black Lab, rode on Gideon's lap; there wasn't enough room for her in the very back with her master's guitar and the plastic buckets and shovels.

"You don't have to sit in the back with the kids," Gideon remarked. "You've got longer legs than I do, so why don't you sit up front?"

"I'll survive the five-minute drive to the cottage," Owen replied. "And besides, I think I'm probably more comfortable back here than you are up there with a seventy-pound Lab on your lap."

"All right. Don't say I didn't offer."

Chuckling, Owen fastened his seat belt. He didn't say it, but watching the youngsters sleeping soothed an ever-present ache, and on the short ride up from the beach while Hope and her cousin laughed about their fun evening, Owen admitted that marriage and fatherhood had given him a sense of purpose he'd lost that day along with Sam and Sean. He had his shop, and the crafting of his sea glass, shell, and driftwood creations gave his mind and hands something to do but couldn't make his heart forget that there was no one to go home to at the end of the day and no one to take care of but himself.

"What the hell is he doing here?"

Hope's sharp question shattered the spell, and Owen peered between the front seats. Parked beside Gideon's Toyota Sequoia in the short driveway of the St. Clouds' cottage was a Dodge pickup with Colorado plates, though Owen didn't need that clue to guess who the truck belonged to; the sudden shift in Hope's demeanor made it plenty clear.

The truck belonged to her ex-husband.

Nine

HOPE GLARED AT DAN'S PICKUP. It was just like him to show up like this, entirely unexpected to cast a shadow over what had been an incredible night.

"I thought you said he wasn't coming out until the end of the month," Gideon said, scowling through the windshield at the vehicle.

"That's what he said." Hope's jaw tightened. "And I'll bet he didn't call ahead to make sure he could get a hotel room."

"I wonder if he did that on purpose."

"He's not staying in the cottage with us. He can sleep in his truck if he wasn't smart enough to make reservations."

When Owen reached from the back seat and

gripped her shoulder in a show of support, she flinched, and it took half a moment to respond and give his hand a grateful squeeze. Still, the warmth in his touch seeped into her skin, and she was able to take a deep breath and stem the rising tide of anxiety.

"Is that offer to sleep on the couch still open for Liam and me?" Gideon asked.

"Yes. Of course."

"Then why don't I give him our hotel room? We've got it for three nights."

"Just so long as you make sure he pays for it."

"Yeah, I'm not that big a sucker, Hope."

She shot her cousin an almost-playful look—one brow and the corners of her mouth lifted. At least Dan's arrival hadn't totally ruined her night. Yet.

"At least not where Dan is concerned," Gideon added. "But I'm learning to be less of a sucker where Hannah is concerned, too."

"Glad to hear it. Can I have your hotel key? And what room number?"

Gideon dug the key out of his pocket and handed it over. "Room number four at the Seacrest Inn."

"Would you like me to take Daphne inside… or would it be better if I waited in the car until your ex is gone?" Owen asked.

She flashed him a grateful smile. "In the car, if you wouldn't mind."

Owen nodded. "One less complication."

"Thank you."

She inhaled deeply and held it for a count of ten, and then let it out as she stepped out of her car, focusing on the warmth clinging to her shoulder from where Owen's hand had rested. It didn't last long enough, and when she tapped on the driver's side window of her ex-husband's truck, her scowl was firmly back in place and the lightheartedness of the evening was fading fast. He jerked upright at her knock; he must've been snoozing. It *was* nearly midnight, after all.

"What are you doing here, Dan?" she asked as soon as he opened the door and rose to his feet.

"I came to see my daughter. I said I was coming."

"Yes… at the *end* of the month. And you were supposed to give me enough time to make reservations for you."

He stuffed his hands in his jeans' pockets and stared at the ground. Narrowing her eyes, she studied him and wondered if Gideon was right. Was his spur-of-the-moment trip just that or had he intentionally come on one of the busiest tourist nights of the year for Sea Glass Cove to guilt her into letting him stay in the cottage with her?

It seemed impossible, but something had changed between them. *She* had changed. She looked at him from a wholly new perspective, unfiltered by fifteen years of marriage and the love she'd once felt for him. She was able to view him and their entire relationship

98

with an objective eye, and his manipulations—whether they were intentional or not—were as clear as the mountain streams near the home they'd shared in Montana. She probably had Owen to thank for that.

The thick lumberjack beard, dark hair, and hazel eyes and the stalky, powerful body attached to them were as familiar as her own reflection, but she *felt* like she was looking at someone she'd met only a handful of times. There was a distance between them that hadn't been there at any point in their relationship, and despite her annoyance, there was enough of her that still cared for him and worried about him that it hurt—a deep ache that might never go away.

"How long have you been here?" she asked, forcing her attention back to the surface.

"A few hours. Where have you been?"

"It's the summer solstice. We were down on the beach with the rest of the town."

"Where's Daphne?"

"Asleep in the car."

"Can I see her?"

"In the morning," Hope replied, surprised by how fast and firmly the response came out. "If you had called ahead, I would've been happy to make sure she stayed awake for you, but since you didn't, I'm not going to wake her up. She's had a very busy day, and she's exhausted."

"Hope…."

"Do you have a place to stay? Or were you planning to sleep in your truck?"

"I tried to get a room for the night, but they're all booked."

She dangled Gideon's hotel key in front of him.

"How did you…?"

"Gideon's here, and he's kindly agreed to sleep on the couch and let you have his room at the Seacrest Inn—room number four. You remember how to find the Seacrest, right? It's at the bottom of the hill before you get to town, first building on Sea Glass Drive."

"I remember where it is, but why don't I sleep on the couch instead? I'd hate to inconvenience your cousin."

"You can either accept the offer of the hotel room or sleep in your truck. But you won't be staying in the cottage with me."

He regarded her with eyes wide, and for a minute as he stared at her in disbelief, she worried he would try to convince her to change her mind. Then he took the key. He was either too tired or too stunned to argue, or maybe it was apparent she wasn't going to back down. All of the above, most likely.

"You'll need to stop in to the office," she continued, "and let them know you're taking the room instead of Gideon."

A car door opened behind her, and she glanced over her shoulder to see Gideon stepping out. He was trying hard not to be obvious, but only a blind man would miss the glances he shot her way as he leaned into the back seat to lift his sleeping son out of the car. It was a barely disguised offer of escape—an excuse for Hope to bid her ex-husband goodnight.

She didn't hesitate to take it.

"I'll bring Daphne down first thing in the morning, and you can spend however many days you need with her. I won't intrude. Gideon reserved the room for three nights, but that should give you time to make arrangements if you want to stay longer."

"Three nights will be plenty for now. I only took a few days off work."

"All right then. We'll see you in the morning."

Dan hesitated, gave Hope one last, pleading look, and slid back in behind the steering wheel.

She waited until his taillights had disappeared before she let out a breath and walked back to her car. With her ex gone, the fight-or-flight rush of adrenaline he had a talent for triggering subsided, leaving her shaky and drained.

"I hate to ask, but could you carry Daphne in, Owen? I'm not sure I can lift her right at this moment."

"I'd be happy to."

The way he said it with that gentleness in his voice told her he truly *was* happy to help. Because he seemed to need the paternal fulfillment as much as she needed his assistance, she let him settle Daphne in bed while she pulled out her daughter's nightgown. He bent over to kiss the girl's forehead, habitually, and Hope's chest tightened. Even after three years, the habits and instincts were as strong as ever, and she could only imagine how much he missed even the simple rituals like putting his child to bed. She watched him with fascination, like she often did.

When he asked where the linens were so he could help Gideon and Liam get settled on the couches downstairs, her fond gaze turned into a disbelieving stare, and she tilted her head to the side.

"What?" he asked, suddenly and endearingly self-conscious.

"You are such a breath of fresh air, Owen. I'm sorry if I sometimes don't comprehend how effortlessly giving you are. Honestly, I can't. I've spent fifteen years having to drag that kind of helpfulness out of my ex, and it's going to be a hard habit to break."

"It's the only way I know how to be." His expression softened immediately, and though he didn't say it, she got the message. *You deserve so much better than you had.*

"I'm getting that. I'm just not used to it. But believe me, I do appreciate it even if I still can't quite believe it's real."

"Put your daughter to bed," he whispered and leaned down to kiss her cheek, "and if you have any energy left after that, we can talk out on the deck for a bit."

Nodding, she turned to her daughter as he left the room. She removed Daphne's sandy shoes. Her clothes were a bit trickier, but it was a testament to how tired the girl was that she stirred only briefly enough to mumble incomprehensible complaints and help Hope pull the Elsa and Anna nightgown over her head. Then she was out cold again, and Hope tucked her in, kissed her forehead, and tiptoed out of the room. She felt a little guilty for not even trying to get Daphne to brush her teeth, but she knew her daughter well enough to know there would be no waking that girl until morning.

Downstairs, Owen and Gideon already had the couches made up and Liam tucked in and as dead-to-the-world asleep as Daphne. Hope hugged her cousin tightly.

"Thank you again," she whispered.

"My pleasure," he replied. "The couch might not be as comfortable as a hotel bed, but the cottage is definitely better... and the look on Dan's face when you didn't give in was the best of all."

"As a precaution, you might want to call down to the Seacrest and let them know of the change of occupant in room number four and—"

"I already did that while we were waiting in the car."

She tightened her arms around him for a moment more. Then she let him go and stepped outside with Owen so Gideon could get ready for bed. They wandered over to the deck railing, and she pulled his arms around her, chilled despite the warmth enduring into the night. Below them, the tide had turned and was crawling its way back toward the dunes, but many dozens of fires still flickered like citrine jewels.

"Are you all right?" Owen asked softly.

"I'm not sure what I am, but I'm going to count tonight as a win because I was able to say no to him without hesitating. That's a step in the right direction for me."

"But he still took away some of your enjoyment of tonight."

"He took away a *lot* of it. Too much."

"I can fix that."

She smiled. Because she believed he could.

"You see all those glittering fires?" he asked. "Remember how much fun we had tonight sitting by ours?"

"Mmm-hmm."

"Good. Hold on to that feeling until you don't *have* to hold on to it. Until that feeling stays on its own."

She kept her gaze focused on the fires and concentrated on her breathing—slow and deep, in and out. The weight of his arms around her was comforting, and as soon as her mind latched onto *that*, there was no forcing her attention back to the fires. But that was okay. She was hyper aware of her body pressed to his, and that awareness drew her focus away from thoughts of her ex and his penchant for disrupting her happiness. As she consciously noted the planes of Owen's body and the heat where they touched, the tension left her and she relaxed into him.

"Better?" he whispered.

"Much." She sighed, genuinely content again. "Your Sam was a lucky woman."

"I like to think we were both lucky." He lowered his head and kissed the curve of her neck. "And I'd like to think that same luck might be smiling on me again."

She turned her face up to his, and the adoration in his eyes melted her heart. "I'd like to think that, too. Owen?"

"Hmm?"

"Would it be too much to ask to spend the next couple nights at your place while Daphne's with her dad? Not tonight but tomorrow night and the night after? Then Gideon and Liam could have the cottage and be more comfortable. I feel like I owe it to them."

"I doubt they think that. And no, it's not too much to ask. I was going to offer, but I wasn't sure you were ready for that."

She swiveled in his arms, and he knitted his hands together behind the small of her back. Standing on her toes, she kissed him long but gently. "I didn't know if I was or not, either, until just now. But now I *know* I'm ready for it. Just so I know our boundaries, is sex on or off the table?"

He chuckled and pressed his forehead to hers. "Why don't we just keep going the way we are and see what happens? One step at a time, darling." He yawned, and with reluctance, he released her. "See you tomorrow?"

"Can't wait."

Ten

"ARE YOU SURE YOU DON'T want to come with us, Hope? I don't mind waiting until you get back from dropping Daph off with Dan."

Hope finished double-checking Daphne's overnight bags, set them by the front door, and turned to her cousin. "I'm sure. I should really get some writing done today while I don't have Daphne underfoot. I've done hardly any writing since we've been here."

"Having too much fun with Owen, huh?"

"That... and I've been unwinding. I thought I was almost back to a place where I can focus on my stories again."

"And then Dan showed up and ruined it like he always does."

She nodded. "But I can't let him do it this time. I *have* to get this book finished. I promise we'll all do something together tonight, though. Maybe have dinner together if you boys are back from your adventure in time."

"By 'all', I assume you mean Owen, too."

"If that's all right with you."

Gideon grinned. "You bet it's all right. You have fun writing."

"Always do when it flows. And you boys have fun… doing whatever you end up doing."

"I was thinking of heading down the coast, maybe showing Liam Devil's Punchbowl, the Yaquina Head lighthouse, and maybe the Oregon Coast Aquarium."

"You think you're going to have time to do all that and make it back in time for dinner? Or should we plan for dinner tomorrow night?" She growled. "I'm really sorry Dan showed up like this. I don't like that Daphne's missing out on time with you guys. She doesn't get to see you often enough as it is."

"Dan showing up isn't your fault, cuz. And we'll be back in time for dinner tonight. Maybe we'll just go to the aquarium. Liam'll probably enjoy that more, anyhow. What time do you want us back?"

"Six-thirty or seven? Owen won't close his gallery until five."

"Six-thirty it is then."

Gideon left the living room to check on their

kids, who were sitting out on the deck waiting for the adults. It was sunny now, but out over the ocean, clouds were gathering and beginning the march toward the coast. The streak of exquisitely clear weather she had been enjoying since she and Daphne had arrived was about to end. The forecasters called for several days of steady rain and blustery winds, and while she was bummed for Gideon and Liam, the prospect of indoor, rainy day activities with Owen was intriguing. What would they discover about each other when they weren't distracted by the beauty outside and didn't have Daphne as a barrier or as glue?

She sighed. There was nothing left to delay the inevitable, and she picked up Daphne's bags, plucked her keys off the dining room table, and headed out the door. As keen as she was for some alone time with Owen, she was *not* looking forward to being separated from her daughter.

"Come on, Daph," she said, walking over to her little girl. "It's time to go. Your dad is waiting, and I'm sure he's got some fun plans for the two of you."

"See ya, Liam."

The cousins embraced, and Hope wished Gideon and Liam could stay longer, that they wouldn't be heading out before Daphne returned to the cottage. One evening together, even as fun as it had been, wasn't enough to last them the months between now and their next visit.

She was surprised to find Dan sitting in the wicker chair on the small deck of his ocean-facing hotel room when she and Daphne pulled up in front of the Seacrest. It was still early yet—just past eight—and in the last few years as the depression triggered by his cycle of failures had gotten the best of him, it had been a struggle for him to rise before ten on his days off. He waved pleasantly as they pulled up, and as soon as Hope parked her car beside his truck, Daphne threw open her door and was out of the vehicle and running up the path toward her father.

"Hi, Daddy!"

"Hi, munchkin." As Hope approached with Daphne's bags slung over her shoulder, Dan smiled at her. "Good morning."

"Good morning," she replied automatically and set her daughter's bags on the porch. "The weather won't hold long, so I won't keep you two. Everything she needs is in her bags, and you have my number."

"Why don't you stay a minute or two?" he asked.

"I can't. I need to get to work."

"Still working all the time, huh?"

Hope frowned. "No, actually. I've done very little work since we've been here, which is why I need to get some writing done while you have Daphne."

"So it's a good thing I showed up when I did."

"No, it really isn't. Not without notice. Showing up like this is always stressful for me *and* for Daphne,

Dan, and I can't keep dropping my life for your every whim. I *won't*."

"Please don't fight again," Daphne said quietly. "I hate the fighting."

"We're not going to fight, baby girl. Give me a hug, and I'll get out of here so you and your dad can get your adventures started." Hope opened her arms, and Daphne launched herself into them.

"Why can't you come with us?" the little girl whispered.

"Because it's your daddy's turn to spoil you."

"But how come we can't all do stuff together like you and me and Owen do?"

Hope sighed and squeezed her daughter tightly, wishing she didn't have to let go and knowing it was futile to think she could soak up enough love in a few moments to last her until she picked her daughter up in two days.

"Someday you'll understand, baby girl. For now, have a good time with your dad and be on your best behavior for him, okay? And you and I and Owen will do something together when I pick you up day after tomorrow. Deal?"

"Deal. I love you."

"I love you, too, Daph. More than anything else in this world. You know my phone number. Please call me tonight, okay? I want to hear all about your day."

Daphne nodded solemnly.

111

Reluctantly, Hope released her. "You heard me, young lady. You be a good girl."

"I will, Mom."

"She's always a good girl," Dan said.

"I know, but it doesn't hurt to remind her. You two have fun."

Her eyes prickled, and she leaned down to kiss her daughter's cheek before turning quickly away before the tears started falling. This wasn't the first time since the divorce that she'd walked away from them, and so far, it wasn't getting any easier. It wasn't just the separation from her daughter that ripped the wounds in her heart open all over again; it was the reminder that the family she'd fought so long to keep together was broken and that, however necessary the decision, she'd been the one to make that final, irrevocable break.

As she drove away, the tears started falling. Silently. She was past the ugly sobbing, at least, but she still hadn't figured out how to stop herself from crying every time, and she wondered if she ever would.

Upon her return to the cottage, she knew at once that she didn't want to be alone. Even with its happy memories, it was too quiet without Daphne. She'd never be able to get any work done here, so she grabbed her notebook, favorite pens, and laptop and headed back down the hill to the Sea Glass Gallery, hoping Owen wouldn't mind her sitting in his office for a while until she got hold of herself. If he did, she'd sit out in the parking area in her car and work, but she doubted that would be enough. She craved his soothing presence.

With the old insecurities coursing through her, she left her work in her car and slipped into his shop. He was talking with customers, detailing how he made the sea glass wind chimes that had first broken the ice between them, and she chewed on her bottom lip while she waited for him to ring up the sale. She admired the ease with which he dealt with his customers and the smiles he lavished on them that would win over even the most miserly client. No wonder he'd been able to make his crafts and his store successful enough to support him and his wife and son. And what was even more amazing to her wasn't his ability to schmooze; it was how natural it was. This wasn't a show he was putting on. It was who he was.

Sensing her watching him, he glanced over, and his smile widened.

"Hi there, gorgeous." With no one else in the shop, he strolled to her, his expression slipping into concern as he neared. "Everything all right?"

"More or less. Dropped Daphne off with Dan, which is never easy. Not because I don't trust him with her—I do—but because…." She shook her head, unable to give voice to the rest of the thoughts as the guilt clamped down on her again.

Owen folded her into his arms. "Shh. I don't need to know."

He held her for a long time, and that and his quiet understanding was enough to ease her heartache. How could two men, both with soul-crushing traumas in their pasts, be so different?

"Do you mind if I write in your office for a while? I didn't feel like sitting in the cottage alone, and the breeze is a little too chilly now to be working outside."

"I don't mind at all, but won't the people coming and going be distracting?"

"Honestly, that busyness sounds quite appealing right now. Too much quiet can be just as bad as too much noise."

He let out a soft huff of laughter. "You writers are a strange breed."

"We really are," she agreed.

"I'll try not to bug you while you're working."

"Somehow, I don't think you *could* bug me."

Chuckling, he said, "Go get your things and I'll grab you a cup of coffee from next door."

She almost purred at the offer and hurried out to her car. Owen had another customer when she returned, but a steaming mug of coffee was waiting on his desk in his office. She briefly contemplated closing the door—out of habit—but decided against it, not liking the idea of even that thin barrier between them. She opened her laptop and then her notebook and glanced over her outline and the last few pages she'd written to refresh her memory of where she'd stopped. With a deep breath to flush the rest of the bad emotions from her system, she jotted notes of what she needed to write next.

Then she started writing, occasionally glancing up to watch Owen with his customers.

It seemed like only minutes had passed when he knocked on the still open door and asked if she wanted to join him for lunch in the Salty Dog or if he should bring her something to eat. Because the words were flowing like they hadn't in a long time, she asked him to bring her a bowl of his mother's mouthwatering clam chowder.

He brought two and sat with her, quietly observing her as she continued to write, stopping now and again to eat a spoonful of chowder. After about fifteen minutes, she looked up abruptly.

"I'm distracting you," he observed.

"No. Not at all," she replied.

"Then why did you stop writing?"

"I just realized that you *aren't* distracting me."

"I don't understand."

"Normally the only person I can stand to have in the room with me when I'm writing is Daphne, and that doesn't usually work so well, either, because she wants attention. I could *never* write when Dan was in the room with me. He could be absolutely still and silent, but his mere presence unsettled me. Especially toward the end."

"So I'm distracting you by not distracting you."

She laughed. "Yeah, kinda."

"Well, since you're well and truly distracted now, finish your lunch so I can take your bowl to the kitchen and let you get back to work."

Because she was anxious to dive back into her story, she scarfed the rest of her clam chowder and handed him the bowl, barely remembering to thank him before she returned her attention to her laptop. She picked up right where she'd left off with no trouble getting back into the rhythm. Her fingers raced across her keyboard, and an energy that had been absent from her writing sessions for months on end crackled through her. She was uninhibited by the fear of being a fraud for writing romance when her marriage had failed, and there were no thoughts of sales or what her readers would think of this story, either.

There was only her and the characters and the pure joy of writing.

When she reached the end of the chapter, instead of stopping like she'd gotten into the habit of doing, she wrote the first few paragraphs of the next chapter to make it easier to pick the story up the next time she sat down to work on it. Then she *had* to take a break. Her eyes were starting to feel funny, and she had the delirious sensation of being stuck halfway between her fictional world and the real one.

And when she looked up, she was shocked to see the sky overcast and a drizzle pattering the windows of

Owen's gallery. She was even more surprised when he thanked his customers, walked them to the door, and flipped his open sign to closed.

"Closing up early?" she asked.

"Uh, no, it's after five."

She glanced at the clock on her laptop and jerked back. It was indeed almost twenty minutes past five. "Wow."

Quickly, she tallied up her word count for the day and was stunned to see she'd written over ten thousand words. She hadn't had a day like that since…. She couldn't actually remember. College, most likely.

"Productive day?" Owen asked as he counted out his till.

"Amazingly so." She stood and stretched. Oh, yeah. She'd definitely been sitting on her backside all day. Every muscle in her body was stiff from hours with little movement, her butt bones hurt, and her knees took some coaxing to straighten. Rolling her head from side to side to work the kinks out of her neck and shoulders, she grinned. "I haven't had a ten-K day in *years*, Owen."

"A ten-K day? What's that?"

"A day in which I write ten thousand words. Even on my more productive days lately I've only averaged twenty-five hundred, maybe three thousand words." She giggled. "I haven't ever been drunk, but I think this might feel a bit like that. My brain's mushy and I'm strangely euphoric at the same time."

"No offense, but you *sound* a little drunk. I'm ready whenever you are. We're supposed to have dinner ready for Gideon and Liam by six-thirty, right?"

"That's the plan."

"Well, we'd best get to it because the meal I have in mind takes a little time to prep. Just let me pop next door…."

She gathered her things and was waiting for him when he returned with a brown paper sack full of… she had no idea what.

"Is that dinner?"

"Part of it," he replied, opening the bag so she could see.

"Clams! What are we going to do with them?"

"We're going to wow your cousin with Mom's famous and top-secret steamer clam recipe."

"If it's top secret, are you sure she wants you sharing it with me? Because I fully intend to help you with dinner. This whole cooking together tradition is fun."

"She's the one who suggested it."

There was some hidden meaning in his words and in the tenderness of his voice, but her brain was too muddled to decipher it. She'd never been much into cooking until adulthood had necessitated it, but she re-membered how fiercely her grandmother had guarded her prized recipes. *You don't share recipes like these with just anyone*, Nana had said. *You only share them with family.*

Eleven

"LORD ALMIGHTY, that was incredible," Hope purred. "I think it was even more amazing than when your mom makes it at the chowder house."

"Well, yeah," Owen said. He picked through the sauce to make sure no one had missed any clams that had fallen out of their shells. Disappointingly, there wasn't a single one left. "This is *the* recipe. To make this in the restaurant, Mom had to make a couple changes, and it's good but not as good as the original."

"Your mom is one amazing cook," Gideon remarked, knitting his hands behind his head and stretching for a moment before he pushed to his feet. "All right, Liam, you and I are on dish duty since Hope and Owen cooked."

Habitually, Owen rose to help Hope's cousin and nephew clear the table, but Gideon shook his head.

"Oh, no you don't. Liam needs to learn that everyone in this household pulls their weight." Gideon eyed his son with one brow lifted as if waiting for the boy to complain.

Liam clamped his mouth shut and took his plate and Hope's to the kitchen without a word.

"Hannah seems to have him convinced that he doesn't have to help out," Gideon explained, "but he's plenty old enough to have a few chores."

"If you're looking for an argument from either of us," Hope quipped, "you're going to be disappointed. Daphne has chores, like clearing the table and helping with dishes."

"And Sean used to help us clear the table, too."

Gideon dropped his head for a moment, then looked sideways at Owen. "I haven't had a chance to say it, but I am so sorry about Sam and Sean. It isn't the same around here without them. Heartbreaking, man. Truly heartbreaking."

Owen nodded in acknowledgement but didn't let those thoughts take root. He was getting better at that. Every day he spent with Hope and her beautiful little girl made it easier and easier. He retreated with her to the living room where they'd started a fire in the hearth, waited for Gideon and his son to do the dishes, and tried to ignore the dull ache of missing his son and the sharper pain of missing Daphne. The little girl had fully ingrained herself in his heart.

As if on cue, Hope's cell phone rang. Glancing at it, she said, "It's Dan's number. Must be Daph calling. Hello?" Immediately, her face brightened. "Hi, baby girl. How was your day?"

Owen rested his head on the back of the couch and closed his eyes. From the one-sided conversation, he gathered that Dan had taken Daphne to the tide pools on Tidewater Point and out to the Stalwart Island Lighthouse as well. Disappointment dampened his contentment. He'd hoped to take her and Hope out in his kayaks to visit the lighthouse as soon as they had a calm enough day to do it, and while kayaking itself might be an adventure for Daphne—and maybe Hope, too—the small but elegant lighthouse was the best part.

"Let me ask him," Hope was saying. "Owen, would you like to talk to Daphne?"

"Is that a good idea?" he asked quietly.

"Dan's in the shower."

"In that case, you bet I want to talk to her." Hope set the phone in his waiting hand, and he grinned as he lifted it to his ear. "Hiya, Daph. Sounds like you've had an exciting day."

"Yeah. It was fun. But I miss you and Mom."

"We miss you, too, sweet pea. Even with your cousins and their dog here—who's staring at me right now like she thinks I have food—it's too quiet without you."

"She's a funny dog. I wish we could have a dog."

"Why can't you?" Owen's brows rose. He couldn't explain why, but Hope struck him as an animal lover, and until Daphne's innocent comment, he hadn't thought to wonder why she and Daphne didn't have any pets.

"We moved too much, and Mom and Dad said it was too hard to find a place to live that would let us have pets."

"Pets do make it difficult."

From the corner of his eye, he saw Hope frown.

"Do you like dogs?" Daphne asked.

"I love dogs. Don't mind cats, either. Birds... not so much. They're loud and messy."

"Then how come you don't have any pets?"

"Sam was allergic to cats *and* dogs."

"How come you haven't gotten a dog or a cat since she died?"

"I work a lot of hours, and it doesn't seem fair to leave an animal home alone so long."

"Couldn't you bring her to your store?"

"Not with it attached to Mom's chowder house. Health inspectors tend to frown on having pets in restaurants."

"Oh." Daphne was silent for a moment, then she said in a low voice, "I gotta go. Dad's done with his shower."

"He knows you called your mom, right?"

"Yeah. But I don't think he likes me talking about you so much."

"I don't imagine he would. It may seem to him like I'm trying to do his job, but I promise I'm not. No matter what happens with your mom and me, your dad will always be your dad. No one can ever take that away from you and him. I'll give you back to your mom so she can say goodnight. Can't wait to see you on Wednesday, sweet pea."

He handed the phone back to Hope and stood, suddenly in need of some fresh air. He slipped out to the back deck and walked over to the railing, hunched over with his forearms folded on it. For almost a minute, he kept his thoughts at bay and watched the storm-driven waves pound the rocks and islands sheltering the cove in eruptions of foamy salt spray. The distraction didn't last, and too soon, doubt churned through him like the water frothing and boiling around the cliffs.

There was one glaring difference between his relationship with Hope and his marriage to Sam. With Sam, love had been simple and uncomplicated. Not so with Hope. Her ex-husband was going to be a shadow on them, and he'd known that from the start, but the reality of it was different than he'd expected. Meeting the man, dealing with him face to face had been his foremost concern, but it wasn't an issue. Not really. Either they

124

would find a way to get along or they'd learn to avoid each other.

Owen didn't want to share Hope and Daphne with the man. Even more than that, he didn't want to feel like he was stealing them from him.

He took several deep breaths, trying to ease the anxiety. It was just the weather. He had a love-hate relationship with nights like this. He loved the raw power of the storms but hated the dark memories they brought.

"Are you okay?" Hope asked, hovering in the open sliding glass door, uncertain.

"Yeah," he lied. "Just thinking we should take a walk on the beach. Storms bring in all kinds of fun treasures."

"But the tide's still up. And it's likely to start raining again any time."

Abruptly, he pushed his troubling thoughts aside and turned to her with a grin. "What? Are you afraid you'll melt?"

Her laughter dispelled the rest of his doubts. It was a beam of radiant sunlight that sliced through the gloom, and when she sauntered over to him, confident and flirty, the clouds inside his mind cleared, burned away by a flash of desire. She folded her arms around his neck and angled her body against his, claiming his mouth with a demand that made him lightheaded. With a will of their own, his hands slid over her hips, gripping her firm rump and hoisting her off the deck. She gripped his waist with her thighs and braced her fore-arms against his chest with her hands locked behind his neck.

"This is about the only good thing about my daughter spending the night with her father," she said huskily. "Maybe after our walk, you and I can get a little frisky. Or *friskier*."

"Maybe we will."

Unwillingly, he set her gently on the deck, pleased when she didn't pull away. But then a fine drizzle began to fall, and he pressed his forehead momentarily to hers with a sigh.

"Looks like we're going to need rain slickers."

Twenty minutes later, Hope was parking her SUV in the vacant northern beach access. Shadow, the black Lab, could barely contain her excitement, and when Gideon walked around to the back of the vehicle to get her, her wiggling escalated into yipping. Owen grabbed his canvas treasure sack and hung it from his shoulder before joining Hope's cousin at the rear of the car to see if the man needed a hand with his excited canine.

"Hush up, you dopey dog," Gideon muttered as he fought to get her to hold still long enough to put her leash on her.

"You could probably just let her run," Owen remarked. "There's no one out here tonight."

"I do that and she'll make a beeline straight for the water. She's a good swimmer, but it's a bit rough out, even for her. And I don't think Hope would appreciate having a salty and stinky wet dog in her car."

"I think you're underestimating your dog's intelligence," Hope remarked.

"Have you met her?"

She ruffled the Lab's ears. "Yes, I have. And she's a smart girl." She waved a stick Owen hadn't seen her pick up. "Come on, Shadow."

The dog pranced at Hope's side the entire way from the parking area through the dunes to the beach, and when she hurled the stick, the black Lab launched after it, flinging damp sand behind her. Owen slipped his canvas sack from his shoulder and held it out to Liam.

"Find me some sea glass and shells and an interesting piece of driftwood, and I'll help you make a wind chime for your mom tomorrow afternoon."

"Dad, can you help me?" Liam asked.

The look on Gideon's face said he'd rather do anything but help make something nice for his ex. It passed quickly, and he bent his head to search the shore for treasures with his son, throwing the stick for Shadow to keep the dog out of their way, out of the water, and occupied.

Hope slipped her hand around Owen's offered elbow, and they strolled lazily after her cousins.

He wondered what it felt like when love turned to loathing. Because he couldn't imagine it. He hadn't ever felt a strong enough connection to any of the women he'd dated before Sam to have developed that kind of anger or whatever it was Gideon held for his ex-girlfriend. Did Hope feel the same about her ex-husband? Not that he could recall. The man set her on edge, but he hadn't ever seen the same disgust on her face as had shadowed Gideon's just now.

"You frown any harder, and your eyes are going to disappear beneath your eyebrows," Hope remarked. "Whatcha thinkin' 'bout?"

"Gideon despises Hannah," he replied slowly. "I can't imagine hating someone I loved like that. Is that how you feel about your ex?"

"I don't think he hates her. Not in such a black and white way. He hates that she let him down. Love is supposed to be a partnership, right? And you and Sam were either lucky enough to find such a partnership or you worked to *make* one."

"Right."

"Gideon didn't have that with Hannah. He was willing to put in the effort to make it a partnership, but she wasn't."

"And... was it the same with you and Dan?"

"Yes. But also much more complicated."

"How so?"

"He *tried* to be a partner. He just... couldn't do it."

Owen waited almost a minute, but she didn't

elaborate. Her expression now was different than it had been this morning when she'd shown up at his store. There was no irritation or panic. Instead, he saw sadness and contemplation.

"Why couldn't he?" he finally asked when it became clear she wasn't going to continue. He didn't like pressing her, fearing maybe it was too uncomfortable for her to discuss, but his curiosity got the best of him. They were at a point that he needed to know more of the details so he knew what he was up against… and how he could be the partner she needed.

"He didn't know how. His parents divorced when he was young, and he was bounced back and forth between them—unwanted and a burden—until he finally left home at sixteen. His father was abusive, and his mother is certifiably nuts. How was he supposed to learn how to love or what a marriage should be from them?"

"Sounds like he didn't have much of a chance."

"No, he didn't."

"But that doesn't mean he couldn't make a choice. We can only blame our parents so long. After a certain point, we have to make a choice to either be like them or to be different."

"That's a fine sentiment," she murmured, "and I agree. But it's not that easy."

"I didn't say it was."

"Those habits that were beaten into him…. They

just run too deep. There are things—thought processes, empathy—that come naturally to most people that he has no idea about."

"Like what?"

"Like how he didn't see the need for him to go to parent-teacher conferences or pick Daphne up from school with me. He figured as long as she had one parent going and doing all that, that was all she needed. And because I was the one who came from the normal home, he trusted me to know and do what was best for her. He couldn't see that I wanted him to be present, that *she* needed him to be. That's not how his mind works. He's never been taught to think like that. I asked him how he felt when his parents didn't show up for his school things, and when he said it hurt, I told him that that's exactly how she feels when he doesn't show up for things. I think it was the first time he'd ever looked at it like that."

"How could he not? It's obvious."

"For you and for me, yes, it is. It's not for him. Pointing that out to him—that was the last chance I gave him."

"Obviously he didn't do what you needed him to with it, or you'd still be married."

"He tried for a while, but those habits were just too strong for him to break. And I couldn't do it anymore. I was losing my mind trying to do everything for all of us, and Daphne was beginning to suffer for it. I think when my sweet little girl started getting sent to the principal's office two, three times a week for hitting other kids or spitting in their faces—acting out at school because she couldn't fix what was wrong at home—that was my wakeup call. I was willing to put up with how he treated me because I could see a good heart buried beneath the lifetime of abuse and neglect, but when it came to Daph...."

Owen bristled. "He was abusive?"

"Never physically. He was actually very conscious to not perpetuate *that* part of the cycle. But verbally, yes. He spoke the way he'd always been spoken to. I'm not defending him, because you're right. We reach a point when we make a choice to act as we do. But I understand why he is the way he is. I guess that's why I stayed so long. I kept hoping he'd make the choice and start taking the steps to be better."

The fine mist that had begun when they'd stood out on her deck began to thicken into a drizzle, and the droplets glittered in her hair. Beneath the gloomy sky with those liquid gems gracing her features, she was more beautiful than ever, with her soul on full display. It took a remarkably strong woman to endure what she had and still be able to see the good in the man who'd put her through it. Suddenly, he didn't want to hear anymore. Didn't want the anguish and regret to shadow her face for even a second more.

He clasped her face and drew her against him,

kissing her hard and deep. It took only a moment for her to overcome her surprise, and then she was kissing him back with her arms locked around his neck.

"You are an incredible woman," he murmured against her lips. "I'm sorry Dan couldn't see it."

"I think he did. He just didn't know how to show his appreciation."

"I'm complimenting you, and you're still justifying his behavior."

"Habit. Sorry."

"Don't apologize for having one of the most amazing hearts I've ever encountered."

"Fine." Sass sparked in her eyes, a brilliant light that sliced through the murk. "I'm not sorry."

He kissed her again, drunk on the radiance of her spirit.

"Get a room, you two!" Gideon called.

"We plan to!" Hope replied with a sexy giggle. "A whole house, in fact!"

And just like that, the darkness had passed, and the same relaxed, go-with-it sense of adventure that had dictated the whole of their relationship so far was firmly back in place. Owen rested his forehead against hers and closed his eyes, smiling. If it weren't for her ex, he'd have no doubts at all about where they were heading.

Twelve

THE HEART OF THE STORM had arrived, and it lashed the coast with gale-force winds and sheets of driving rain that endlessly pattered the windows. The violence of it was, in its own way, as beautiful as any sunny day. Hope watched the waves crash as she chopped the ingredients for a hearty beef stew while the boys worked out in Owen's garage finishing the wind chime for Hannah. Not only was stew just the kind of comforting, hearty meal to warm the body on a cold, blustery night, it was also quick and easy to make and even quicker and easier to clean up.

Gideon and Liam had to leave early in the morning, so they would need to pack their bags tonight, and Hope fully planned to put the quiet evening to good use. She'd asked Owen to pick up condoms on his way home from work, and while they'd decided to let things happen as they would, that was something she was going to *make* happen. Sleeping beside him last night, snuggled close to his side, had awakened a voracious desire. At this point, there was only one thing that would scratch that itch, and tonight was the last night they'd have alone together.

Now or never, she affirmed, tossing the stew meat in flour and dropping the chunks in the pan with the butter and onions she'd already set on the heat. Her lips twisted in amusement. *Well, it's either now or we'll have to wait for who knows how long.*

When the stew was simmering away on the stove, she sat at his dining room table to watch the storm hurl wind, rain, and waves at the coast. She'd brought her laptop with her, but she didn't think it was a good idea to try to write right now; she was likely to get lost in the story again like she had yesterday and this morning and forget to stir the stew. Since she was trying to do something nice for Owen and Gideon and Liam, burning dinner wouldn't do. As soon as it became clear that it was going to be a choice between writing and wondering what Daphne and her father had done together today—which then turned her focus to how much she missed her daughter—she rose and brought her laptop into the kitchen. Maybe if she set her computer on the counter near the stove, she'd remember to stop periodically to stir.

It seemed like only a few minutes later that the boys returned noisily from the garage, but when she glanced at the clock on her laptop, nearly twenty minutes had passed. Crap. Quickly, before they noticed she'd neglected her duty, she stirred the stew. Fortunately, she had the heat low enough that the stew wasn't yet sticking to the bottom of the pot.

"That smells amazing, Hope," Owen said, sliding his hand around her waist as he joined her at the stove. He kissed her neck. "How about I take over so you can get back to your writing?"

She swiveled in his arms, tilting her head.

"Why are you looking at me like that?" he asked.

She shook her head and started to say she wanted to do something nice for him, but she knew him well enough to know he'd say she already had, so she just smiled, grateful he understood that she needed to write. Figuring he and her cousin would want a taste to hold them over until the stew was done, she pulled two spoons out of the silverware drawer and held them out.

Gideon snatched the spoon before Owen had a chance to comprehend what she was offering. He dipped it in the stew and groaned with delight as he slurped his first taste. "Oh, God, this is good, Hope. It's even better than Nana used to make."

"I doubt that."

"I don't," Owen said after he'd tasted it. "It's delicious."

More than a little pleased with herself, Hope grinned. "Just wait until the flavors have had more time to simmer together."

Grabbing her laptop, Hope retreated to the living room. At some point, Owen came in and started a fire in his fireplace, but she was only vaguely aware of the saturating heat of it and the occasional crackle and pop, too entrenched in her work to notice her surroundings. She surfaced from it long enough to enjoy dinner with Owen and Gideon and Liam and accept the praise they lavished on her, but as soon as they got up to clear the remnants of the meal and wash the dishes, she dove right back into her book.

Finally, it was time to say goodbye to Gideon and Liam, and it was harder than she'd thought it would be. They'd had such a great visit, and it reminded her of all the fun they'd had here as kids and of how much she missed them both. It had been far too long since they'd gotten together like this.

"Come back out again this summer if you can make it," she whispered as she hugged her cousin.

"I think I will, even if I have to turn down a job or two to make it happen. This was the best visit you and I have had in years, Hope."

"I agree."

"Divorcing Dan was the right decision," he said. "I know it doesn't always feel like it, but I can see it was."

"Thank you. You two drive safe tomorrow. And call me when you get home so we can plan your next trip."

Gideon shook Owen's offered hand and then pulled him in for a hug. "It was great to see you again."

"Likewise. Good luck with the custody battle, and be sure to call me if there's any way I can help."

"I will. Thanks, man."

Hope gave Liam a big squeeze, and then Owen did. Then the boy and his father were walking out the door into the storm.

She tucked her arms around Owen's waist and watched out the window as her cousin and his son raced out to their car and disappeared into it. She missed them already. "I think if Gideon and Liam and Christian and his family lived here full time, I'd never want to leave Sea Glass Cove again. I love Montana, but there's something here I've either never found there or lost sometime in the last fifteen years."

"It *was* good to see them again. And easier than I thought it would be."

"Is that why you hadn't seen him since before Sam and Sean died?"

She expected him to deny it, but he nodded.

"I never meant to, but I avoided him whenever he came out these last three years." He turned away from the front door and wandered into the living room.

Flopping on the couch, he said, "Now I wish I hadn't."

She plopped beside him with her feet tucked under her and her knees resting on his thighs. With a hand against his far cheek, she turned his face toward her. "No thinking like that tonight."

"I'm not thinking like *that*. I promise. I was actually thinking that I could've gotten to know him better and that it would've been nice to have a male friend through everything. Even a part-time one." He chuckled. "I love my mother and my sister dearly, but sometimes their attempts to help did the opposite. Red was great, and honestly, I don't know where I would've been without him, but he's a dad. It's not quite the same. And his sons were still in that stage of carefree youthful stupidity, and they had no idea how to help."

She regarded him with a pointed look and one brow raised. "Uh, hate to break it to you, but yeah, you are thinking like *that*. So knock it off."

"Sorry. It's the storm. Days like this, it's hard not to think of those days after…." His voice trailed off when he met her stern gaze, and then he laughed. "Yes, ma'am. I'll knock it off."

"Thank you."

He leaned in and kissed her, and seeing her opportunity, she took it. She slid onto his lap and threaded herself around him, deepening the kiss and combing her fingers through his hair. When he groaned, she smiled against his lips and dared to take it a step farther. She slid her hands down his neck, chest, and belly, slipped them under his lightweight fleece pullover and T-shirt, and then pushed her hands back up to his neck slowly, tantalizingly. His eyes closed, and a frown drew his brows together. The way the muscle in his jaw twitched made her pause.

"Everything all right?"

"Yeah…."

"But…?"

"It's been a while, remember?"

"So?"

"I don't want to rush it. I want to savor it."

"Well, even if we rush it the first time—it's been a while for me, too, you know—we have all night to slow down and savor it." She rocked forward to kiss his lips. "Besides, I don't want to slow down enough to start thinking about it. It's been a long time since I've really *wanted* to make love. For years, it's been one more chore."

"How on earth did you manage to stay in that marriage as long as you did?"

"A combination of stubbornness, empathy, and hope."

"Sounds about right. Wait here."

He lifted her off his lap and settled her on the couch, then left her alone in the living room. Minutes ticked by, and the only sounds in the room were the occasional pops from the fire and the opening and closing of closet doors drifting down from upstairs. What was he doing?

Moments later, her question was answered when he returned to the living room with an armload of pillows and blankets and dropped them on the floor.

"My mama always said there's no substitute for romance," he said. "So if you're sure this is what you want, I figure there isn't much that's more romantic we can do on a night like tonight than make love in front of the fire."

"Your mama's a wise woman."

She helped him make their nest in front of the fire—close enough to enjoy the heat of it but far enough away that they weren't in danger of a spark igniting their bedding. There was only one kind of heat she wanted burning the sheets, and it wasn't the literal kind of fire. When they'd arranged their blankets and pillows to their liking, she turned to him, resting her hand against his cheek. Then she leaned forward and kissed his lips.

"In answer to your question a moment ago, yes, I'm sure I want to do this." She threaded her arms around his neck and pressed her body against his. "There are few things recently that I've been more sure of."

With a speed and intensity that took her breath away, he claimed her mouth, digging strong fingers into her back and pinning her to him. Desire thrummed through her, and as he trailed kisses from her jaw to her shoulder, she quivered and gave in to the desire in a way she hadn't in years. If ever. In this moment, she was his and he was hers, and there was nothing else in the world but the surge of sensations melding with emotion. She arched back and let her body do the begging, and a wholly different sensation enveloped her—a deep, rejuvenating bliss that felt a lot like love.

Thirteen

HOPE'S MOTHER HAD OFFERED her a piece of advice shortly after she'd first started showing an interest in boys, and she had thought she was following it when she married Dan. Last night, Owen had proved her wrong in the most incredible way possible—thoroughly, with a physical attentiveness that matched his instinctive emotional generosity.

Some men can turn you into a puddle of mush, and some will make you feel like the strongest, most desirable woman in the world. Find one who can do both... at the same time.

Dan had made her feel both at one point or another but never both at the same time, and she hadn't realized that until she'd met Owen. She hadn't *fully* realized it until last night. She had never in her life felt so weak and so strong simultaneously, and it was intoxicating.

They'd lazed in bed well into the morning, deciding that with the soupy fog clinging to the coast a walk on the beach wasn't nearly as appealing as snuggling together, so now, a quarter past eleven, they were finally finishing breakfast. As soon as they washed the dishes, it would be time to head down to meet Dan at the ice cream parlor to pick up Daphne. She couldn't wait to see her daughter, but she was in no hurry to see her ex again.

"You ready to go?" Owen asked. He put the last dish away.

"As I'll ever be. Are you sure you want to come?"

"I'm positive. I've loved our time alone together, but I miss—"

"That's not what I mean."

Endearingly, he took her face in his hands and kissed each cheek and then her lips. "I can handle your ex. Besides, he's always going to be a part of Daphne's life, so I'm likely to cross paths with him at some point."

Hope only nodded in acknowledgement. A queasiness built in her gut, and she stepped into the bathroom to wash her face before they left. Staring at her reflection in the mirror, she muttered, "You're delaying."

She jerked away from her reflection and followed

Owen out to her car. Why was she so nervous about him meeting her ex-husband and vice versa?

"It'll be fine, Hope," Owen said.

"Didn't know you were a mind reader, too."

"Don't have to be with that face. Take a deep breath and relax, all right?"

She nodded and did as he suggested, but it didn't help. Not much, anyhow. When he reached over and squeezed her hand, that helped more.

Then she was pulling into the Delta Mall shopping plaza and Dan's truck was parked in front of the ice cream parlor and there was no time left to calm herself.

"Daphne's spotted us," Owen remarked when she made no move to get out of the car. "See?"

Hope returned her daughter's wave, and at seeing her little girl's brilliant smile, joy overpowered her anxiety. She only had to talk to Dan long enough to hear how his visit with their daughter had gone, and then he'd be on her way, and her life would return to its new and peaceful rhythm.

"That's more like it," Owen commented gently. "Come on. Let's go satisfy our sweet teeth. And then we can have some ice cream after."

It took a moment for his quip to register in her brain, and when it finally did, she grinned up at him. "You make everything so much easier," she replied. "Thank you."

He dipped his head in acknowledgement and held the door open for her.

Dan and Daphne hadn't ordered their ice cream yet, and by the looks of things, they'd arrived only moments before Hope and Owen. There was the expected awkward silence as Dan eyed his ex-wife's new companion, and Hope had to force herself forward to make the introduction.

"Dan, this is Owen McKinney. He owns the Sea Glass Gallery, and his mom and sister own the Salty Dog Chowder House next door to it," she said. "Owen, this is my ex-husband, Daniel Andrews."

Owen extended his hand, but it was almost two seconds before Dan stood to shake it.

"Pleasure to meet you," Dan greeted, his voice clipped.

"Likewise," Owen replied lightly. "May I get everyone's ice cream so you can have a chance to talk?"

Hope glanced sharply at him, wishing she could beg him to stay, to give her an excuse to cut her time with Dan short. Instead, she sucked in a breath and said, "That would be great. Thanks, Owen."

"Can I help?" Daphne asked, tugging on his hand. "I know what my mom and dad like."

"Sure, sweet pea, if it's all right with your parents."

Hope nodded. As they walked away toward the counter to order the ice cream, she heard her daughter whisper to Owen, "I missed you."

The man's entire countenance lit up, and he winked. She couldn't hear his reply, but she was certain he told the little girl that he'd missed her, too.

"So that's Owen," Dan remarked.

"Yep." Hope turned back to him.

"Daphne talked about him a lot. Almost non-stop."

"He's great with kids."

"Sounds like it. Are you two...?"

She waited for him to finish, and when it became apparent he wasn't going to, she said, "There's definitely something there. What it is I don't know yet, but I don't have to know." She stopped short of telling him that it was nice being with someone whose motives and actions she wasn't constantly questioning and testing. "It's enough to know that I'm healing and that I have more of myself to devote to Daphne."

He stared at his hands, fiddling with his truck keys, and Hope tensed in anticipation of what was coming.

"I'm sorry, Hope." His voice cracked and tears welled in his eyes. "I wish I wasn't so broken. I wish I could be a better father to Daphne. I wish I could be what you need. I tried. You have no idea how hard I tried to change, but I am what I am."

She squirmed, hating him for tugging on her emotions even as her heart broke for him all over again.

Several times she opened her mouth to reply only to snap it closed again. For a long time, they stared at each other, and all the words they'd said or couldn't say hung between them, a thick fog of regret and mourning.

"I love you, Hope."

"You may not believe this, but I still love you, too, Dan, and I will always care deeply about you." She sighed. How many times had they had this conversation in the months since she'd told him she needed a divorce? "I didn't leave because I stopped loving you. I left because I had to. Because I did everything I could to help you and it only ended up breaking me. I can't help anyone if I'm broken, too."

He nodded and wiped at his eyes. "I should go."

"No, stay and have an ice cream with your daughter."

He shook his head, rose from his stool, and hurried away.

Hope didn't watch him go. She folded her arms on the table and rested her forehead on them, staring blindly at the salt-and-pepper flecking that was too close for her eyes to focus on even without the tears blurring her vision. Frustration and heartache melded in a blistering concoction, and she wasn't sure if she wanted to cry or scream. Once again, he'd wound her up and left her abruptly to figure out which direction was up while the earth was still spinning. How long would it be before she stopped letting him do this to her?

The worst part of it was that none of it was intentional. If his manipulations were a conscious tactic to control her, they'd be easier to fight. But they weren't, and while her mind doubted that, her gut was certain. They were the habits and learned defenses of a man who hadn't been taught or shown compassion until it was too late. And she had too much empathy. She'd been drawn to him, needing to fill his empty well with love and compassion. But the well was bottomless and no matter how much of herself she poured into it, she could never fill it. And it had nearly destroyed her. As it was, it would be a long time before she broke the habits.

Sensing that she was no longer alone, she dried her eyes on her arms as discreetly as she could and forced a smile. Daphne was seated at a table near the door with her father, and it was only Owen who joined her. And he wasn't fooled. He saw right through her false cheerfulness.

"I'm fine," she said automatically. When he lifted a brow, she corrected herself. "I'll *be* fine."

Mollified for the moment, he handed over her ice cream—mint chocolate chip in a waffle cone, her favorite—but while she ate it, she felt his eyes on her.

If Dan's well of compassion was an endless sinkhole, Owen's was a spring overflowing. She only hoped she hadn't become like Dan with a crack in her well that drained the waters as quickly as Owen could fill them. She couldn't do to him what Dan had done to her. But at least she didn't *feel* like that.

Well, she hadn't, until seeing Dan again. She glanced at her ex, noted how quickly he ate his ice cream. It was as if he couldn't get out of here fast enough and not even his daughter's love could hold him here. Her jaw clenched, and she scowled.

"Do you mind if Daph and I cancel our beach date with you?" she asked. "I need to go for a drive."

"Do what you need to do. We're still on for dinner, I hope."

Relief trickled through her, though she had no idea whether it stemmed from his understanding of her need or from his desire to keep their dinner date even though meeting her ex-husband probably hadn't been a cakewalk for him, either. Then she shrugged and decided it didn't matter. "We are absolutely still on."

Fourteen

OWEN COVERTLY WATCHED Hope and her ex-husband while he waited for the young woman behind the counter to scoop their ice cream. Beside him, Daphne bounced on her toes, oblivious of the tension between her parents. That was something of a miracle because he felt it from across the room. It bored into him like needles hooked up to an electrical current.

"What does your mom like?" he asked her when the server handed him Dan's banana split.

"Mint chocolate chip in a waffle cone," Daphne replied. "Same as me."

"That's my favorite, too."

She beamed up at him. "Really?"

"Yep. And it's my favorite because it's *my* mom's

favorite."

"I like your mom. She's…. What's the word? It's kinda like funky."

"Spunky?"

"Yeah! She's spunky."

"That she is," Owen agreed with a chuckle.

His amusement faded when he glanced at Hope again. She looked like she was about to cry, and when he shifted his gaze to Dan, he saw why. He caught snippets of their conversation, but he didn't have to hear the words to know what the man said. The agony on both their faces revealed a conversation of lingering but shattered love. It was the same look he remembered seeing on his mother's face when she'd told him and Erin that they were leaving their father, their family, and their home. He cringed. The way Dan looked at Hope, his eyes pleading…. It was a punch to the gut.

"Here you are, Owen," the server said.

He yanked his gaze away and smiled at the woman. "Thanks, Lulu. What's the damage?"

"Fourteen even."

Holding two ice cream cones in one hand, he somehow managed to free a twenty from his wallet and told her to keep the change. Just as he turned toward their table, Dan rose abruptly, and panic and then despair washed across Hope's beautiful face. When the man strode away, she dropped her head onto her arms.

"Got your ice cream," Owen said as Dan passed

him.

"What?" Dan asked dumbly. Then he glanced at the banana split Daphne held out to him. "Oh. Thank you. I wish I could stay—"

No, you don't, Owen surmised.

"—but I need to leave."

"Daddy, please stay," Daphne said quietly.

"I have to go, pumpkin."

Owen noted the panic in the other man's eyes— like a wild animal looking for escape. He started to walk away, but Daphne grabbed his free hand with tears glittering in her eyes.

"Please don't leave me!"

"I'll never leave you, baby," Dan replied. "But I have to get on the road."

"You can't stay long enough to eat some ice cream with your daughter?" Owen asked a little more sharply than he intended.

The other man eyed him warily, his jaw tightening and untightening like he was fighting the urge to punch Owen. He shifted his weight from one foot to the other, paralyzed by indecision, and Owen's senses heightened, waiting for the fight even as dread settled over him. The man was built like a tank, and while he wondered with a primal curiosity what his chances were of holding his own against Hope's ex, there was no way he'd give in to it. Not in front of Daphne. He'd let the man knock him out without lifting a fist to defend himself because that was better than letting her see him engage in a useless territorial brawl.

At last, Dan straightened, and the fight left his eyes. Resignation replaced it. "I suppose I could."

"I'll take your mom her ice cream, sweet pea," Owen said to Daphne. "You enjoy a few more minutes with your dad, all right?"

"Okay," she replied, brushing her tears away and watching her father like she didn't trust him to stay.

Annoyance stiffened Owen's gait as he walked over to Hope's table. What kind of man would rush away from his daughter when she so obviously wanted to spend a few more minutes with him? Even as he thought it, he knew why. He supposed, face to face with the woman who had broken but still owned his heart and realizing that she wasn't his anymore, he'd have a hard time sticking around to let that pain spear him, too.

He wasn't surprised when Hope asked to cancel their plans to walk the beach so she could take a drive to cool off. At least she still wanted to come to dinner with him.

Dan was the first to leave, but the goodbyes he exchanged with Daphne were easier than they would've been if Owen had let him leave when he'd wanted to. Owen walked out to Hope's car with her and Daphne and declined the offer of a ride home. He grabbed his canvas sack out of the back, kissed her and hugged Daphne, and then watched them drive away. When they were out of sight over the ridge of North Point, he crossed the highway and headed through the dunes to the beach.

The tide was out, so he scavenged lower down the beach than he'd been able to lately and was rewarded with several large pieces of abalone shell and some nice chunks of indigo glass. He could already envision the projects he'd make with them.

While his walk was successful in terms of his work, it wasn't so productive for clearing his head. By the time he reached the rock arch and passed beneath it to Hidden Beach, he was no closer to untangling the thoughts and emotions Hope's conversation with Dan had stirred.

He sat on the bottom step and set his sack beside him.

There was obviously a lot of love left between them, and the guilt that had prickled him earlier returned, digging its talons deeper into him. What if Hope had made a mistake? Sure, she'd said she was still game for dinner with him tonight, but that didn't mean she wasn't second guessing her divorce. In her place, he would be. The look on her ex-husband's face when he'd said he still loved her....

Owen thought he was going to be sick. He knew all too well the shattering pain of losing his wife and child, but his family was forever beyond his reach. Dan's wasn't. For the last three days, Dan's family had been close enough to hold. How torturous that must be, to have his family right there in front of him but to be unable to reclaim them. And then to meet a man not only hoping to move into his place but already doing so….

Owen propped his elbows on his thighs and scrubbed his hands through his hair.

Maybe it was too early to be sure, but he loved Hope and he loved her daughter. And no matter what, he craved their happiness even if that meant letting them go.

"Quit overthinking it, McKinney," he muttered, pushing to his feet.

He climbed the long staircase to the path above, deciding somewhere along the way that he didn't want to wait at home for Hope and Daphne to return from their drive. He needed a distraction, and even creating new products to sell wasn't going to do the trick; there was too much quiet in his garage. Back at home, he grabbed a few tools and supplies and headed to his gallery.

"Whoa, what's the frown for, big brother?" Erin asked as soon as she spotted him strolling into the chowder house. "I guess that meeting the ex didn't go so well. Did he threaten to bury you in an abandoned mine if you hurt his daughter?"

"He didn't say more than a few words to me."

"So… what's got you all twisted up?"

Owen shook his head, not sure if he could adequately voice his concerns. "Would you mind bringing me a bowl of chowder?"

"Sure thing."

Moments later, she returned with his soup and sat quietly beside him while he ate almost half of it. Finally, he couldn't stand her intense stare any longer. He pushed his bowl away. Taking that as an invitation, she curled her hands around his arm and rested her head on his shoulder.

"Don't leave me again," she murmured, sounding far too much like Daphne had not so long ago. "Not now when I am so close to having my brother back again."

"I've never left, sis."

"No, but you haven't been *here* for a long time, either."

"I'm sorry. I am. I never meant to push you away, Erin."

"I know you didn't. It would've been easier to handle if you'd done it on purpose." She sighed. "I'm not trying to make you feel guilty, Owen. I just don't want you to close up again, and I don't know what happened with Hope and her ex today, but I can see you fading a little. What happened?"

"I thought...." He stopped, swallowed, and started again. "Up to this point, she's seemed so confident about her divorce. That's not the right word, but I got the impression that it was a relief."

"And suddenly that's changed?"

"There's a lot more left between them than I realized. And Daphne would be better off with a whole family instead of a broken one."

"Were we better off as a whole family?"

"No, but our family was broken before the divorce and became whole after."

"Who's to say that isn't the case with theirs, too?"

"You didn't see and hear what I did, sis."

"I don't have to know what they said. She left him, Owen."

"Yes, she did. But he needs her, and I think in some way she still needs him. And Daphne needs her father."

"So? She'll be getting an amazing father in you if you and Hope decide to go that route."

His heart lurched with that particular thought, but he ignored it. What his heart wanted didn't matter if Hope's didn't want or need the same. "If Hope needs to fix her family, it'd be selfish of me to stand in the way of that."

"I think you've earned the right to be a little selfish, Owen. Besides, if her ex had done what she needed him to, he wouldn't be her ex."

"Yes… and sometimes it takes the kind of gut check he got when she filed for divorce to make people see what they stand to lose if they don't change."

"Did Dad change after Mom divorced him?"

"How would I know?"

"Believe me. He hasn't. Last Lauren heard of him, he was in court for another DUI."

"I didn't know you and Lauren kept tabs on him."

"We don't. But Uncle Howard went off about it the other day. Guess our dear ol' pop called him up to beg for bail money."

"I assume Uncle Howard told him to take a flying leap off a high cliff."

"Yep. Wish he'd actually do it. The world would certainly breathe easier without him in it."

Out of habit, he nearly chided her for being cruel, but their father didn't deserve his generosity and he certainly didn't deserve hers, so he kept his mouth shut. While he knew Erin was trying to encourage him by using their father as an example, Hope's decision to leave her husband wasn't nearly as simple as their mother's had been. The physical safety of her person and of her children was an easy choice for Andra to make. There was far more room for doubt when it came to emotional security.

"Owen, please stop thinking like this. Have you asked her what she's feeling?"

"No. I haven't had a chance."

"Then you have no proof of anything, and all you're doing is giving yourself an ulcer."

He hugged her tightly. "What would I do without

you?"

"You'd be a miserable only child."

Chuckling, he smoothed his hand over her hair like he had so many times when they were little and she'd been scared of their father's erupting temper or his friends' drunken impropriety. "Right you are."

"Since you're in the mood to admit I'm right, how about you take it a step further and admit I'm right about Hope, too?"

"Fine. You're right about Hope, too."

"Ah," Erin purred, leaning back in his arms. "I could hear that all day and I don't think I'd ever get tired of it."

"Don't you have a job you need to get back to?"

Laughing, she slipped out of his embrace and stood. "Hurry up and finish your chowder so I can take your bowl back to the kitchen."

"Yes, Miss Bossy Britches."

To spite her, he took his time eating his chowder, and she got tired of waiting. He hoped she was right and that his doubts were unfounded, but he couldn't shake the guilt. Still, Erin *was* right about one thing. It was useless to worry until Hope gave him an irrefutable reason to. So he would try to ignore it.

Fifteen

AFTER ANOTHER FOUR-DAY ROUND of wind and rain, Hope was glad to see the sun again. She'd spent much of the day out on the deck of the cottage writing by hand while Daphne alternately read books and built elaborate cities with the set of wooden blocks her father had given her during their visit.

If she was relieved to see the sun, she was even happier to finally feel the last of her anxiety over Dan's admissions slipping away. A picnic dinner on the beach with Owen, some sand castle building, and plenty of scavenging the shore for treasures washed in by the storms were sure to lift her the rest of the way out of it.

With that thought, she smiled and checked her watch. Then she closed her notebook and hooked her pen in its wire spiral.

"Time to demolish your empire, baby girl," she told her daughter, fingering a lock of the girl's silky hair that had pulled loose from her twin French braids. She hadn't realized how many pale gold highlights the sun and salt air had coaxed from both Daphne's tresses and her own until they'd indulged in a mother-daughter hair-braiding party this morning. They looked like proper coast girls now.

"Is it time to go down to the beach already?" Daphne asked, distracted. With her tongue protruding between her lips and a deep frown of concentration pinching her brows together, she set a final block on top of the tower that was as tall as she was. The whole thing wobbled in the soft sea breeze, but after a moment, it stilled, and she stood back with a triumphant grin. "Can you take a picture? I wanna show Daddy."

Indulgently, Hope grabbed her phone and snapped a picture of her daughter with her creation. She sent it off to Dan and was surprised when he replied immediately. "Your dad says, 'great job, Daph.' Want me to video you knocking it down?"

"Yeah!"

Hope started recording and nodded to her daughter. With a shriek of delight, Daphne gave a grand impersonation of Godzilla, crashing through the structure and sending the colorful blocks flying in all directions. Hope couldn't help but laugh at her daughter's antics.

"All right, baby girl. Let's get this picked up quick. We don't want to be late for our date."

It didn't take them long to stow all the blocks back in their handy zipper case and gather the buckets and shovels for building sand castles. Owen was supposed to meet them down at the beach around four-thirty—right at low tide—and he'd volunteered to bring dinner fixings with the thought that they'd have a repeat of the summer solstice even if it would just be the three of them.

His truck was nowhere in sight when she parked in the northern beach access lot, so she figured she and Daphne had beaten him here, but when they reached the beach, he already had a fire going in the rock ring they'd used for the summer solstice. A wide grin split her face when he glanced over his shoulder and rose to greet them. She hadn't gotten to see him nearly enough these last four days; she'd been writing like a thing possessed and, with his one employee out of town for her sister's wedding, he'd been stuck manning his gallery.

She slid easily into his waiting arms and sighed contentedly. "That's much better."

"Mmm," was all he replied as he kissed the top of her head and let out a breath.

Then he lowered his head and kissed her. It was different than any kiss they'd shared, and in the moment before it drove all thought from her mind, it felt like he was trying to memorize every detail, savor every taste and texture.

"Wow," she breathed when he reluctantly released her.

She expected a smug gleam to ignite his green eyes, but she saw only adoration and something she couldn't name—something that sent a shock of anxiety through her. He smiled, and whatever it was vanished. Not sure she'd seen it, she shook her head and drew a deep breath to invite serenity to return.

"What's for dinner?" she asked brightly.

"Nothing fancy. I thought cheese burgers might be a nice, relaxing change from the more elaborate dishes we seem to have a habit of putting together."

"Cheeseburgers actually sound fantastic."

"We've got a while before the coals are ready. What should we do while we wait?"

"Sand castle!" Daphne cheered.

"Sand castle it is." Owen tossed another log on the fire and emptied his canvas sack on the soft sand. When Hope dropped her sand castle buckets and shovels beside his, he laughed. "Looks like we're going to be building a mighty palace this evening."

"Yeah!"

"You should've seen the tower she built with the blocks her dad gave her," Hope remarked as Daphne gathered an armload of the buckets and raced to the damp sand halfway down the beach toward the water's edge. "Grandeur seems to be her theme of the day."

163

"I'll bet it was spectacular."

Hope glanced at him when his voice hitched, but his expression was as relaxed as it ever was. "It was. Are you all right?"

"I'm fine. Why?"

"I don't know. You sound… tired, maybe?"

"It's been a long week."

She was likely overanalyzing because of that kiss moments ago, but she sensed an evasiveness in his words. Then he nodded toward her daughter and flashed her a mischievous grin that said *race you*, and her worries evaporated. She sprinted after him, but she had no hope of catching him, not with his long legs and her much shorter ones.

She was still a tad on edge from her encounter with her ex-husband. Her time with Owen had been so wonderfully unhurried and candid that she had forgotten how tense her every confrontation with Dan was. The old habits were back in place. That's all this was.

As they constructed a massive sand castle together and decorated it with shells and sea glass and pebbles like they had that first, smaller castle what now seemed like a lifetime ago—had it really been only a few weeks?—Hope made a conscious effort to break those old habits.

It wasn't easy.

She couldn't help but note Owen's every smile, listen to his every word and search for the underlying thoughts and emotions, and it frustrated her because it seemed like he wasn't as relaxed as he usually was. There was an intensity about him that felt alien. And a hint of the old sadness, which she now realized had been significantly lessening in their time together, was back, shadowing those beautiful eyes now and again even as he indulged her daughter.

Once her mind, trained by fifteen years of shouldering criticism and blame that wasn't rightly hers to bear, latched onto that, she began to realize that it hadn't only been their busy schedules that made it seem like they hadn't been together as much. There was an emotional distance, too, and there had been since Thursday. Since Owen had met Dan.

Because it was subtle, she didn't say anything, still unsure if it was real or if it was only a figment of her imagination.

After dinner, they hunted for sea glass and shells, and Hope was able to forget her concerns again for a while. Owen found a nice large piece of abalone shell, and when he described how he would use it in a wind chime—as the wind catcher that would knock the striker against the rods—his face lit up. She loved how animated he became talking about his work with Daphne.

Finally, he sat in the sand near the fire and patted the spot in front of him. Hope snuggled herself in and leaned against him with her back pressed to his chest. She pulled his arms around her and watched her daughter dance with the rising tide. Occasionally, she glanced down at Owen's hands as he turned the piece of abalone shell around and around.

All was quiet on the beach tonight. There were a few other parties scattered around, but it seemed everyone else was of the same mind to enjoy a peaceful evening.

With their bodies pressed together, it was impossible to miss when Owen's stiffened beneath her and he stopped turning the shell. She glanced up at him and noted a distant look in his eyes as he stared across the cove toward the open ocean. When she saw the muscle in his jaw tighten, she sat up, twisting her body to face him. She wasn't imagining it this time. "What's wrong?"

"Nothing."

"Doesn't look like nothing. And that *nothing* sounds just like the one I used to give Dan when he asked if I was upset and I lied to keep the peace because it was easier than telling him what I really felt."

At the mention of her ex, a strange light sparked in his eyes—bright pain entwined with guilt.

"Ah. This is about Dan."

He didn't answer, didn't meet her gaze, and it was all she could do to stop herself from begging him to contradict her.

"You haven't been the same since you met him," she said quietly. "At first, I thought it was just me falling back into old habits of overanalyzing everything, but it isn't."

The only indication that he'd heard her was the narrowing of his eyes, which remained trained on some point far away that only he could see.

"What I can't figure out is why."

At last, he brought his attention in close, but instead of looking at her, he lowered his gaze to the shell in his hand. He began turning it around again. Slowly. Methodically.

"He still needs you," he murmured. "Dan. I think he's finally realizing what he lost, and I've tried so hard to ignore it. But I can't…."

She waited for him to continue, but he seemed incapable of putting his thoughts into words. "You can't what?" she asked.

"I lost my family, and it nearly killed me, Hope."

Finally, he met her gaze, and she jerked back. The pain in his eyes was as raw and fresh as it might have been that night he'd gotten the call telling him his wife and son were dead, and it seared a hole in her core, at once white hot and as cold as the darkest Montana winter night.

"I can't do that to him. I can't take his family from him. And I can't do it to you and Daphne. Oh, God, Daphne." His voice cracked at that, and a wild hopelessness claimed his face. "Her voice when she begged him not to leave, and her eyes…. I can't watch her heart break like that and know that I'm part of the reason for it."

"You aren't the reason at all. And believe me. That isn't the first time he's broken her heart. He broke it every time he figured one parent was all she needed at her parent-teacher conferences or to pick her up from school. He broke it every time he turned her away when all she wanted was to play Legos or blocks with him."

She lunged to her feet and hugged herself tightly, shivering as the cooling night air hit her where his body had warmed her.

"Our family was broken *long* before you came into the picture, Owen," she said. Her chin wobbled traitorously. "Broken beyond repair."

"Did he ever *truly* realize what he stood to lose before? You might be surprised what a man will do when he loses everything. What he might do with one more chance."

"I have already given him fifteen years of chances. How many more chances does he deserve?"

Owen didn't answer that, and she didn't expect him to. She was the only person on this earth who could answer that question, and she had. When she'd filed for divorce.

"He will never change. I've lost count of the number of times he's proven that. I spent so much energy and so many years of my life trying to fix a man who won't be fixed. Do you know how many times we moved because the next town, the next job, the next whatever might be better? Montana, Wyoming, Colorado, Washington, back to Montana. I stopped counting after ten. He can't keep a job more than a year—two at most—because he sabotages every relationship he's ever had. At the slightest hint of trouble in any job or friendship, he's done. He finds reasons why it can't work, and sometimes they're reasons that don't exist!"

By now she was shaking.

"After fifteen years of destroying myself over what *he* needed, I have no chances, no strength, no *anything* left to give him." Bitterness and hurt swelled in her chest, pushing her frustration ever higher until it now threatened to spill out her eyes. "L-leaving him was about w-what *I* needed."

Suddenly unable to utter another word, she whirled away, hastily gathered her daughter's plastic buckets and shovels, and called Daphne to leave.

"But Mom!"

"It's time to go."

Hope wiped her eyes and straightened her spine, and when her daughter reached her, she had managed to smooth her expression enough that Daphne only regarded her with a confused frown.

"It's getting late," she explained.

"Can I say goodbye to Owen?"

She almost said no, but instead, she nodded, curious to see how the man would react to *that*. He didn't disappoint. He plastered a smile to his face—it had no hope of reaching his eyes, but she applauded his effort—and returned the hug Daphne gave him. When the little girl asked what they were going to do tomorrow, he said she'd have to ask her mom. If only Dan had been so generous when Hope had told him she was leaving.... He would've proved Owen right. Would've proved that he truly wanted to change and that he *could* change. But he hadn't.

Daphne trotted back to her mother and took her offered hand, sensing something was off but too young to grasp what. Hope wondered if maybe they shouldn't cut their summer vacation short and head home to Montana. Then she dismissed the thought. Running from pain was her ex-husband's mode of operation, not hers, and she had enough of her own bad habits to break without picking up his.

She stopped and glanced back at Owen. He sat with his knees drawn up, his arms draped loosely around them, and his head hanging in defeat. When he curled his arms around his head, she hesitated. She wanted to stride back to him and hug him until their pain went away. Until he realized how much he meant to her.

But she couldn't. She *wouldn't*.

She was done fighting to keep people who couldn't or wouldn't fight to keep her in return.

Sixteen

EVERYTHING IN OWEN SCREAMED at him to follow her, but he couldn't move, paralyzed by the sharp, stabbing pain in his chest. If he hadn't felt it once before, he might've thought he was having a heart attack, but he knew it was only his heart splintering again.

He *had* tried to discredit his fears about Hope and Dan, but the harder he'd tried, the more tightly they had constricted him and the deeper those doubts had reached, dragging up memories that terrified him.

Hope's words made sense, and somewhere in a far corner of his mind that the shadows couldn't reach, he understood that a woman like her never would've resorted to divorce unless there was no alternative left. But, trapped in the thrall of his memories, he was unable to forget that moment in the ice cream parlor when he'd recognized that same black, endless agony in the eyes of her ex-husband. He understood exactly how shattering it was to lose his family and what it could drive a man to do… what it had driven *him* to do.

He shivered, unable to feel the warmth of the summer sun. He was caught in those frigid gray waves again, tossed around by the stormy current.

Grief and guilt and frustration churned together, building and building until it exploded out of him in a bellow. It echoed off the rocky cliffs to the north, and when it died away, quiet reigned and even the ceaseless rhythm of the waves seemed subdued.

Slowly, he uncurled his arms and lifted his head, wincing at the aches that had accumulated in his body from being locked rigidly in the same position. He had no idea of the passage of time, but the fire had burned down to a bed of hot coals. With stiffness in every joint and muscle, he rose and picked up the largest of his plastic buckets and headed down the beach to fill it. It took five trips to fully douse what remained of the fire. Then he picked up his things with a methodical listless-ness, shoved them in his canvas sack, and headed to-ward the arch and Hidden Beach once he was satisfied the fire was totally out. He was in no hurry to go home to his empty house to face the older memories of his wife and son or the newer ones of Hope and Daphne, but the tide was coming in, and it wouldn't be long before he'd be forced to walk around the long way.

When he passed beneath the arch, he habitually checked for abalone shells but as usual there were none. As he climbed the stairs toward the path, he felt like an old man, his joints creaking and stiff, his heart tired of the pain. He reached the top and stopped, frozen by indecision. Involuntarily, his gaze was pulled toward the St. Cloud cottage, and the sight of the glowing lights from within brought a fresh round of despair.

An invisible force drew him out onto the point of rock that formed the arch between Hidden Beach and the main beach. The rocks were fractured, and climbing out across them was only for the foolhardy. He hadn't been out here in three years, and when he nearly slipped, it occurred to him that he'd been lucky to make it out to the point that day without falling. That day, the rocks had been slick with rain and salt spray tossed up by the crashing, storm-driven waves.

He sat in the same spot he'd occupied that day and set his canvas sack beside him. This evening, the sky was a clear, pale yellow as the sun reached for the horizon, and the surf lapped gently at the rocks. Bracing his hands on his knees while his legs dangled over the edge, he inhaled deeply, held it for as long as he could, and let it out, enthralled by the water foaming lazily far below him. As calm as the ocean was tonight, a jump from where he sat would still be dangerous. There were rocks hidden below the surface, and the current swirled around them strong enough as the tides moved to drag even a strong swimmer like him down to the bottom.

"I'm lucky to be alive," he murmured.

The thought came with a rush of relief but also with gratitude, and he sat up a little straighter and opened himself fully to the memories in a way he hadn't ever done. He allowed himself to feel again the crushing grief that had driven him out onto this point in the middle of an unusually powerful storm and to remember how utterly empty he had been standing atop the rocks as the wind buffeted him and how the icy current had embraced him and dragged him under. He acknowledged the miracle that had propelled him smoothly between the point and the tall rocks that had once been part of it. And he thanked Sam and Sean and everything holy for the abalone shell that had been the first thing his hand had touched when he'd dived under the waves after it became apparent that the ocean wasn't going to do the job for him.

He glanced down at his hands. He'd latched onto that shell as if it were a lifeline. No, not as if it *were*. There was no doubt in his mind about that. It *had been* a lifeline, a message from his wife as clear as any ever shouted at him.

You must live!

He'd pushed toward the surface and battled the current toward the beach and dragged himself up onto the cold sand. He'd lain there with the shell clutched in his hand for a long time with the grit digging into his cheek and the rain pelting him, and at some point as his body temperature dropped, he'd had the real epiphany. In trying to die, he was devaluing his wife's and son's lives, and right then he had promised them he'd fight for his life and hold on to their love and the wonderful memories they'd made together and honor their lives by doing so.

Shivering so hard his teeth chattered, he'd begun crawling toward the sand dunes and the highway beyond. He hadn't made it more than two dozen yards when Red had found him. What his mother's beau had been doing out on the beach in that weather, Owen still didn't know. Some would call it luck, but he knew it was Sam's doing. Red had driven him home and stayed with him until his body temperature had warmed to normal. He hadn't once asked how or why Owen had ended up lying on the beach soaking wet, nor had he mentioned the incident to Andra, whom he'd been dating only a couple months at that point, but Owen was certain the man knew.

He scrubbed his hands through his hair and over his face and was unsurprised when they came away wet. He wiped the tears away and his lips twitched. Not quite a smile, but a hint of one.

And then movement out of sync with the waves washing gradually higher up Hidden Beach caught his attention. At once, disbelief washed through him.

There was no way….

Scrambling to his feet, he snatched his sack and stumbled back across the rocks to the stairs. He raced down them, keeping his eyes on the object. When he reached it, he hesitated, not trusting his eyes. Then he reached for it, and his hand clamped on a familiar shape.

An abalone shell.

It wasn't chipped from being knocked against the rocks or pitted by countless tiny organisms like the shell he'd found that day three years ago, either. This shell was pristine, and its perfect iridescent interior shimmered in the warm glow of sunset.

"You've got to be kidding me, Sam," he whispered, awed.

He sat heavily in the damp sand at the water's edge, staring at the shell in his hand. With his fingers splayed, the tips of his thumb and pinky didn't quite reach the edges.

The message was undeniable.

Fight for her.

But he shook his head. He'd done the right thing. As much as it hurt him—and dear God, it hurt—he had to let Hope go. Even if, as she said, there was no possibility of reconciliation with her ex, building a firm, cordial friendship with Dan was going to be difficult enough without Owen complicating it.

Silly man, he swore he could hear his wife say, *that's not your choice.*

176

A wave washed up over his feet, soaking him up to his waist, and suddenly, he laughed at the utter absurdity of it all. He felt as if his sanity had finally fractured beyond salvaging, but at the same time, everything came together with a breathtaking clarity. Is this what it felt like when sanity *returned*?

He stood and shook the clumps of wet sand from his saturated shorts. Before he turned back to the stairs, he tipped his face to the sky, closed his eyes and smiled. And he took the next step in the healing process, one he realized now he'd been afraid to take until he'd met Hope.

He said goodbye to Sam and Sean with a promise to not only fight to stay alive but to *live*.

Because the life he wanted to live included Hope and her daughter. And he couldn't give himself fully to them while he was holding on to a love that was lost to him.

Seventeen

HOPE WATCHED OWEN crest the stairs to Hidden Beach and pick his way carefully out to the point over the arch, and for a terrifying few moments, she thought he might jump. Then he sat, and she forced herself to turn away. She folded her arms across her chest, consciously keeping them loose.

Her emotions had run the gauntlet over the last hour since she and Daphne had left Owen on the beach, and she'd only just managed to subdue them. Seeing him out there on the point.... Her heart thumped wildly again.

"Daph, what do you think about heading home to Montana early?" she asked, drawing the curtains closed so she wouldn't be tempted to watch him. She couldn't let him distract her right now. Sliding into the chair at the dining room table beside her daughter, she added, "Maybe we could swing through Colorado on the way back and you could spend a couple days with your dad."

"I don't want to. I like it here," Daphne replied, half-distracted by her crayons and coloring book. "And you said we could spend the whole summer here."

"I know I did, but…."

Hope snapped her mouth closed, unable to come up with a reason to leave early. She could say she need-ed to get back to work, but the truth was she'd been more productive in the last week here than she'd been in months back home. And she couldn't exactly tell her daughter that she wanted to leave because Owen had let Dan get to him. Daphne wouldn't understand that.

Abruptly, Daphne sat up and looked at her moth-er. "Are you mad at Owen?"

Was she? Not exactly, but he'd hurt her when he'd questioned the solidity of her decision to divorce her ex-husband. "No, baby girl, I'm not mad at Owen."

"But when I hugged him goodbye, he was sad. And you're sad, too. Is it because of Daddy?"

"It's complicated." Frowning, Hope wished she hadn't put her head down at the ice cream parlor. She wished she could've seen what had transpired between Dan and Owen and Daphne. What had Dan said?

"I'm sorry, Mommy."

"What do you have to be sorry for, baby girl?"

She hugged her daughter tightly. "This isn't your fault! This is just grown up stuff that has nothing to do with you."

"But it might. I told Daddy about all the fun things Owen does with us. Like building sand castles and having fires on the beach and cooking dinner with you. I like watching you cook with him. You're so happy. I don't think he liked me saying that."

"You told your father that?"

Daphne nodded. "He said he was happy for you, but I don't think he meant it."

"Do you...." Hope swallowed, choking on the words. "Do you still wish your dad and I were still together?"

For a long time, Daphne didn't answer, and just as Hope was beginning to think she was going to start crying and beg her to take Dan back so they could be a family again, the little girl stunned her.

"No. I miss him, but he pays more attention to me now. And you're happier. Especially with Owen. Will you marry him?"

Because it was probably best to make the cut now, she sighed. "Owen's a friend, baby girl."

Daphne shook her head. "You kiss him like you used to kiss Daddy."

Hope snorted. She'd *never* kissed Dan like she kissed Owen, and the comparison made her squirm with longing. She barely contained the whimper.

Her daughter's expression turned dreamy. "You kiss him like they kiss in the movies."

Was it getting hot and stuffy in the cottage, or was it just her? Hope stood and kissed the top of her daughter's head as she passed by on her way to the French doors. It was a warm night out, and a little fresh sea air sounded like just the thing to help clear her mind. Besides, the sun should be setting by now, and having the curtains closed suffocated her soul. When she pushed over the thick curtains covering the French doors, she let out a shriek.

Owen stood on the other side with his fist raised to knock.

Without thinking about the consequences, she opened the door... but slowly. "What are you doing here?"

"You weren't expecting me," he observed, his eyes rounding with uncertainty.

"No, I wasn't."

"I owe you an apology. And I figured it would be best to give it to you sooner rather than later." He lowered his gaze. "I screwed up, Hope, and I'm sorry. I let old memories scare me."

She stared at him, hearing the words but unable to comprehend them. "What?" she asked dumbly.

"May I come in? Or would you rather come out?"

"Uh...." She glanced over her shoulder at Daphne, who watched her with curiosity. "Come on in.

Daph, would you take your coloring book up to your room for a bit while I talk to Owen?"

"Can't I stay?" the little girl asked. "Owen?"

"Listen to your mom. This may not be the kind of conversation you want to hear, sweet pea."

With a dramatic sigh at being interrupted, Daphne gathered her art supplies and took them upstairs. Hope stepped back to let Owen in and briefly considered closing the door, but now even more than before she needed the fresh evening air. He eyed her warily, and the shimmer of pain in his gaze tugged at her heart. Not trusting herself, she wandered into the kitchen and filled a glass with iced tea. She offered it to him, but he shook his head. She leaned against the counter and folded her arms across her chest.

Tilting her head, she realized he'd changed his shorts since she'd spotted him out on the rocks, and at once, she noticed the abalone shells in his hand—one pristine and perfect, the other chipped and pitted. Noticing the direction of her gaze, he lifted them so she could see better.

"Why'd you bring your abalone shells?" she asked, more than a little curious.

"To help me explain why."

He was quiet for several moments as he stared at the shell.

"Why what?"

"Why I said what I did tonight. Why, for a moment, I couldn't see anything but how much your leaving hurt Dan. And why I put Dan's needs before yours."

Her mouth fell open, and his lips curved in a humorless, self-deprecating smile.

"That surprises you," he remarked.

"Yes. It does."

"What about it surprises you?"

"That you're so... self-aware. And so willing to admit it."

He set the perfect shell on the counter behind him and handed the other to her. She skimmed her fingers over its ragged outer surface and caressed the chips around the edge. The interior was still smooth and beautiful, though, undamaged by the tides and organisms.

"You asked me once how losing Sam and Sean didn't break me. And I said it came close," Owen said. "You remember that? I think it was our second date."

She caught her bottom lip between her teeth. That conversation was burned into her brain, and she doubted she'd ever forget it. Nodding, she continued her inspection of the shell and waited for him to continue, sensing that this shell had an important role in whatever he needed to tell her.

"I lied. It *did* break me."

Her head snapped up, and for almost a minute, she stared into his eyes. The only time she'd ever seen anyone as vulnerable was the moment when Dan had reminded her of all the ways he'd changed… and she'd told him it wasn't enough and asked for a divorce. She winced with that thought, and shook her head. No, not even in that moment had she seen anyone lay their soul so bare as Owen's was now.

"The darkest day was about a month after the accident," he continued, his voice so low she had to lean closer to hear him. "I hadn't made it in to work at the gallery for almost a week, and I couldn't bring myself to build anything new to sell. I just sat in my house, staring at the walls, sometimes feeling nothing, sometimes feeling too much. That day…."

He shook his head and the muscle in his jaw worked, and it took every grain of willpower Hope had to resist crossing the distance between them to hug him.

"I remember catching a glimpse of myself in the window or a mirror, and I didn't recognize myself. I saw that same wild, haunted look in Dan's eyes at the ice cream parlor. It's the look of a man who's lost everything. His wife. His child. His will to drag himself out of bed every morning. His reasons for staying alive. Except that Dan still has the tiniest shred of hope. *That* is what I couldn't un-see."

His voice had turned rough, so she took another glass out of the cupboard and filled it with water. This time, he accepted it and drained half of it in a single swallow.

"That's why I pushed you away tonight. Because I know what it's like to completely lose hope. I couldn't get past the fact that I was snuffing his last spark of it. I couldn't see that it was already lost because you wouldn't have filed for divorce if there was any chance left that he might still become the man you needed him to be."

There was a lot more to his story, so she grabbed her glass of water and the ragged shell and gestured for him to join her at the dining room table. She held on to the shell, letting her fingers alternately play over its rough exterior and slide around its smooth interior. Frowning, she gave in to her curiosity.

"Owen... what happened that day?"

"It was stormy, like it's been for the last week. Just... black. For days on end. And the ocean was about as rough as I've seen it. I don't know if the weather played a role, but it certainly didn't help."

He fell silent, his eyes locked on the abalone shell in her hands without seeing it. The way he retreated into himself—into his memories—scared her.

"I wanted to die. To be with Sam and Sean again. So I walked out onto the point over the arch... and I jumped."

She'd expected the answer, but hearing him say it sent a shockwave through her. However confused and hurt she was by his rejection earlier tonight, she reeled at the thought of this beautiful, compassionate man not only having the urge to end his life but acting on it. She pressed her fist to her lips and listened. Her writer's mind had no trouble visualizing what he described, and she was as surprised as he was that he hadn't been smashed to death on the rocks.

"Then I felt this on the bottom," he said, reaching for the shell she still held. She set it in his hand, and as he stared at it, a faint fondness eased some of the heartache. "And I swear, I heard Sam calling me, telling me I had to live."

He told her everything that happened after that, and by the time he finished his tale, the tears were streaming down her cheeks. No matter where their relationship headed, she vowed she would track down Red and thank him. Even though Owen had made the decision to cling to life by that point, he hadn't been out of danger. She had no doubt that he'd had hypothermia, and if Red hadn't found him, he might've succumbed to it and died right there on the beach.

"I was ready to let you go. For his sake. And then I thought I had to let you go for *your* sake because you need to build a stable relationship with him and you wouldn't be able to do that with me around."

"And what do you think now?"

He picked up the other shell, and his demeanor shifted as he handed it to her. His smile was sad, but it had a touch of whimsy. "That it's not my choice to make."

"Isn't this Sam's shell? The one you found when you met her?"

His smile widened, and he shook his head. "This is the third I've found now."

"You found this *tonight?*"

"It washed up on Hidden Beach right about sunset. And it's yours."

"No, I can't take it. Finders, keepers."

"Hope. It's yours."

She lifted her gaze from the shell and inhaled sharply. He held her gaze, and she understood in a way she would never be able to put into words that he indicated something far deeper than simple possession when he said *it's yours*. It was hers in the same way that first shell he'd found was his wife's. The same way the second was his.

"I don't know if you can forgive me for considering your ex-husband's needs before yours," he said slowly, releasing her gaze and standing. He picked up the abalone shell he'd found the day he'd jumped off the point. "But if you can, I'll never make that mistake again. That's a promise."

He stepped around the table with such quiet grace that she didn't notice until he pressed a kiss to her cheek.

"As much time as you need to decide, take it. I'll be waiting."

And then he was gliding toward the open French

doors and out into the deepening twilight before she'd recovered enough wits to call after him. He didn't return, perhaps sensing that she needed time to think about everything he'd said.

Hope returned her gaze to the abalone shell. She wanted to forgive him. Compared to everything he'd survived and everything she'd endured in her marriage, his actions earlier tonight were only a minor offense. But even if she did, where did that leave them?

There was something else she'd been having too much fun to give much consideration to, but when he'd pushed her away, he'd forced her to address it.

She and Daphne were only here for the summer, and come mid-August—only a month and a half away now—they'd be on their way home to Montana to get ready for school.

"Mommy?"

Hope looked up and spied her daughter peeking around the corner. The wide-eyed expression made her wonder how much of her conversation with Owen Daphne had heard. Most of it, probably.

"Come here, baby girl."

"Is Owen okay?"

"He is now."

"But he wasn't."

"No, he wasn't."

"He is now 'cause he found you."

"I don't know about that, my love."

"I do. Are you going to forgive him for making you mad tonight?"

She started to explain that she hadn't been mad but hurt, but she didn't have the energy left to clarify. So instead, she said, "I think so."

"Does that mean we can stay here in Sea Glass Cove with him and be a family like you and me and Daddy used to be?"

The question blindsided her, and for almost a minute, Hope couldn't answer. Other than in those first few weeks after Dan had moved back to Colorado, Daphne hadn't begged her to let him come back like a lot of kids did when their parents separated. And not more than an hour ago, she'd said she liked that Dan paid more attention to her now when it was just the two of them. Hope groaned. She'd also asked if Hope was going to marry Owen. How had she forgotten that?

Finally, she managed to choke out, "It's not that simple, baby girl."

"Why not? He makes you smile, and you make him smile. Big, bright smiles like the sun is shining inside you and you can't keep it all inside." She tilted her head and studied Hope with her eyes narrowed and her lips pursed. Then, hooking her arms around Hope's neck, she asked, "That's love, isn't it? Do you love him?"

Hope opened her mouth to dismiss her daughter's question, but she couldn't say that no, she didn't love Owen. She couldn't even say she didn't know because she *did* know.

She loved him.

But she'd also loved Dan—still did—and she was jaded enough to know that love wasn't everything.

All she could offer her daughter was another vague non-answer. "I don't have any answers tonight, baby girl. I have a lot to think about. And it's your bedtime."

"Mommy?"

"Hmm?"

"Can I sleep with you tonight? I don't want you to be alone."

Laughing softly, Hope stood and picked her daughter up, holding her close. "Yeah, you can sleep with me tonight."

Eighteen

AFTER A FULL DAY OF WAITING, Owen began to wonder what else he needed to do to convince Hope he was sorry and would never again devalue her needs. After the second day without seeing her and Daphne, his promise to give them space and time to consider his apology and decide if he deserved a second chance had crumbled. He'd walked by the cottage to see if they would like to join him for an evening stroll on the beach, but they hadn't been home. By lunchtime on day three, he'd completely rearranged the wind chimes and other sea glass, shell, and driftwood items in the front windows of his store, dusted the entire gallery, restocked all the toys, and ordered more to replenish his stockpile in a mostly useless effort to distract himself, and he now sat at the counter beside his register. He tapped his fingers on the shell he'd found at the bottom of the cove and watched a couple in their early sixties browse the shelves.

The longer he went without talking to her, the harder it became to not think about her and the more certain he was that he couldn't let her go.

"You coming over for lunch, or would you like me to bring it to you in here?"

Owen almost fell off his stool and swore under his breath as he turned toward his mother. "Uh, I'll come get some in a minute. Soon as my customers leave."

Andra's brows rose. "You're a tad distracted again today, I see."

"That's the understatement of the decade."

"Still haven't heard anything from Hope?"

He shook his head. "She wasn't home last night."

"I hope she didn't up and head back to Montana early."

"I don't think so. The windows on the cottage were all open, and her laptop was sitting on the desk in the den. She probably took Daphne down for ice cream."

"I didn't think she was the kind to leave without telling you. She's considerate, no matter how mad she might be. She's got a kind heart, that woman."

"She does," Owen agreed, tracing random patterns over the shell's smooth interior.

Andra studied him with eyes narrowed, watching his hand hover over the shell.

Telling Hope about the day he'd found it had let loose a flood and given him the courage to finally tell his mother and sister about it and to decide that he wouldn't keep the shell and what it represented hidden away anymore. After they'd hugged him and cried, a weight Owen hadn't been aware of had lifted, and when Andra threatened to rip Red a new one for not telling her, he'd had to fight not to laugh at her indignation. It had taken him longer to talk her down than it had to tell her he'd jumped off a cliff, but by the end of the evening, they had regained the closeness they'd lost as a family when Sam and Sean died. He'd sat on the couch with Erin on one side of him and their mother on the other and talked far into the dark hours of the morning about moving to Sea Glass Cove, about his wedding, about Andra meeting Red, and about a thousand other happy memories including several more recent ones involving Hope and her sweet daughter.

"She's done a lot for you in a short time," Andra said, following the direction of his thoughts. Or maybe she'd been thinking the same ones.

"Yes, she has. She's a remarkable woman. And the more I think about it, the less I can empathize with her ex-husband."

"You know what they say about things like this,

don't you?" she asked. "If you can't stop thinking about it, don't stop fighting for it."

"I don't plan to, Mom," he replied. "I'm just not sure how long I should wait before I make another attempt. And what do I do if she's decided I'm not worth the hassle?"

"You show her you are." Andra joined him behind his counter and wrapped her arms around his shoulders.

"And if that's not enough?"

"Then she's not as remarkable as she seems to be. You're a good man, Owen, and a good woman will see that."

"You're my mother. Your opinion is biased."

"Maybe so, but Sam knew it. And you know even better than I do that she was a good woman."

"She was the best."

"And you think Hope is in her class, or you wouldn't have fallen for her like you have."

He nodded in agreement, and let out a sigh that was half chuckle. "Surprisingly, this conversation is *not* making the wait any easier. I'll be over for lunch in a few, Mom. Thanks."

Giving him another squeeze, Andra left him to tend to his customers. The woman had fallen in love with his latest wind chime, the one he'd made the first day after his talk with Hope—the one with the wind catcher he'd made from the large round abalone shell fragment he'd found before he'd opened his mouth and shoved his foot in it.

"Do you find all the items you use right here in Sea Glass Cove?" she asked.

"I do sometimes stray south to Angel Beach for the glass—it doesn't get picked over as much—but yes, most of the pieces I use come from Sea Glass Cove's beach. All the pieces for this particular wind chime did and just the other day."

"Oh, how fun. Honey?"

Her husband pulled out his wallet with an indulgent smile. "How much?"

Owen quoted him a price, rang up the sale, and stepped into his office for a box and tissue paper. While he was wrapping it, he watched them from the corner of his vision. Those private smiles gave the impression of new love, but the way they held each other and moved in an effortless dance—at one with each other—spoke of a much older, stronger love.

"How long have you been married?" he asked as he finished wrapping the wind chimes.

"Forty wonderful years tomorrow," the man replied. "We're here for a second honeymoon. Thought I'd take the old girl out to the lighthouse."

"That's where he proposed," she added, beaming at him. "So long ago, but it feels like yesterday."

The love that glowed in their eyes made Owen's heart ache. "Congratulations on your longevity, and I wish you a very happy anniversary."

He walked them to the door and watched them drive off. Then he headed into the Salty Dog for lunch, sitting at the counter on the stool nearest his store like he always did so he could keep an eye out for any customers who wandered in. Andra spotted him and brought him a plate of fish and chips, and he turned his back to the restaurant to enjoy it, trying and failing to discourage thoughts of Hope. The love emanating from his customers just now had brought her forcefully but pleasantly back to the forefront of his mind.

He'd waited long enough. Tonight, after work, he'd go over to her place and talk to her, and if she wasn't home again, he'd wait on the deck until she returned.

"Hey, big brother."

Owen closed his mouth with a sigh and set his fork on his plate. Erin propped her hip on the stool beside him as she often did, and he regarded her with a brow raised. "I'm beginning to think you take some kind of perverse pleasure in interrupting my lunch. Maybe I should start eating in my office."

"Whine, whine, whine," she quipped.

She'd made the exact same retort the day he'd met Hope, but if he thought *that* reminded him of it, what she said next *really* did.

"See that pretty woman at the table by the window?"

"Which window?" he heard himself ask.

Erin's face split in a wide grin. "Like you need to ask."

He didn't. Without seeing her, he sensed who the gaze he felt on him belonged to. Slowly, he turned on his stool, drawn instinctively and helplessly to her. She and her daughter sat at the same table they had the day he'd met them, and when his eyes met Hope's across the room, his lips curved with a will of their own. Yeah, he'd never be able to let her go now. Not even if she wanted him to.

"Go get her, Owen," Erin whispered, giving his shoulder a squeeze.

He rose and caught his sister's wink as he started toward the woman and her daughter who'd dragged his heart out of the cold, lonely sea. Hope was the beach, and an invisible current propelled him toward her, his smile widening as her face brightened the closer he came. Then he saw the shell he'd found and given to her sitting on the table, and his heart plummeted.

"Hi," she said shyly when he reached her.

"Hi," he echoed, uncertain.

In contrast, Daphne could barely contain her excitement at seeing him again, and she launched herself into his arms without waiting to see if he was ready to catch her.

"Missed you," she whispered.

"Missed you, too, sweet pea," he replied, hugging

her tightly. "More than you know."

"Baby girl, would you go ask Erin to bring Owen's lunch over? And take your time please."

"Sure!"

The little girl dropped out of his arms and trotted across the restaurant to Erin. Hope gestured for Owen to sit across from her, and his invitation for her and Daphne to join him in his usual spot at the counter died on his lips. They couldn't face each other at the counter.

"It's good to see you again," Hope began. "At last. My daughter isn't the only one who's missed you these last few days."

That was promising. "Well, that's good, because she's not the only one I've missed."

"Thank you for giving me the time and space to think about everything I needed to consider." She lowered her gaze to the shell. "Daph and I have done a lot of driving and a lot of talking, and I've done a lot more thinking."

"And?"

"And... you're right to be afraid for Dan and to make me aware of how he felt."

There was no spark of vindication, only regret and worry. If he was right about that, had she decided he was also right that she needed to give her ex-husband another chance? Half an hour ago when he'd told his mother he would fight for Hope, he'd been so sure he'd try no matter what, but already a crack had formed in that resolve. He wanted to fight for her, but if she didn't want him to, how could he hurt her like that?

"That's part of why I stayed as long as I did," she continued. "I was terrified that he'd kill himself if I left, but I don't think I ever thought about it quite like you made me see it."

"How did I make you see it?"

"As something that isn't mine to own. And once I realized that, I saw that that fear was another way he was controlling me even after our divorce. Admitting that makes it easier to set and keep my boundaries with him. I called him yesterday and told him that he needs to make prior arrangements when he wants to come see Daphne, just like I'll make my own when I take her to see him. And I set a few other boundaries with him while I was at it and told him what Daphne and I planned over the last few days for our future."

"That's great, Hope," he replied. "You need that."

"Yes, I do. And about this shell…." She picked it up and skimmed her fingers over it almost lovingly. "It's not mine to keep."

"Yes, it is." He searched her eyes, hoping to see something—anything—in them to contradict her words, to tell him she hadn't decided to reject him. There was only a faint contemplative frown. Feeling more fractures forming in his heart, he dropped his gaze to the shell. Suddenly, he understood that if she wanted to close the door on their relationship, it wasn't his right to try to keep it open. He cared about her enough—*loved* her enough—that her happiness was more important than his… and that he would do anything to make her happy, even if that meant walking away. "Give it back to the ocean if you don't want it."

"The ocean can't have it, either. Owen, look at me."

He did, prepared to see sadness in her eyes. Instead, a grin brighter than the clear day outside lit up her face and hummed throughout the rest of her like she couldn't contain it. He tilted his head with eyes narrowed, confused.

"It's not mine to keep," she repeated, "because it's *ours*."

Half a second. That's all it took for her meaning to sink in, and when it did, he shot off his stool and reached for her even before he slipped around the table. Clasping her face in his hands, he drew her off her stool and against his body and kissed her firmly in front of a restaurant of people who cheered and clapped. His mother and sister watched from behind the counter with Daphne, and all three grinned like Cheshire cats.

"Ours," he breathed against her lips. Then he grinned. "That's something I can't wait to get used to."

She hooked her arms around his neck and leaning back to beam at him. "Um, there's one more thing I need to tell you, but I told Daphne she could do it."

Hope waved Daphne over, and the little girl eagerly complied. "Can I tell him now, Mom?"

"Hold on just one more second. So, one of the things Daphne and I have talked about at length and investigated these last few days was when we need to go back to Montana. And the answer is...." Hope gestured to Daphne.

"We don't!" Daphne cheered. "Well, not to stay."

"You're staying in Sea Glass Cove?" Owen asked, certain he must be dreaming.

"We're staying in Sea Glass Cove. In the cottage for now," Hope confirmed. "We'll make a trip back to Montana to put the house up for sale and sell what things we don't want to bring, and.... Um, we have a favor to ask."

"Anything."

"Gideon called this morning. He's going to be out for most of August, and Daph and I thought—if you're willing—we should give him the cottage. Give him a chance to feel like he's home, if only for a few weeks. He broke the news to Hannah that he plans to seek full custody of Liam, and as you can imagine, she's not taking it too well."

"I'm sure she's not, but Liam will have far more stability with Gideon. As to you two staying with while he's here, I am willing *and* eager," Owen replied. He laughed and glanced over his shoulder at his mother and sister. "You owe me, Erin!"

She stuck her tongue out at him but her smile

didn't fade.

"What's that about?" Hope asked.

Chuckling, he pressed his forehead to Hope's. "She knows."

"Are you glad we're staying with you, Owen?" Daphne asked, slipping her arm around his waist and her mother's.

"Glad is not nearly strong enough to describe what I am," he replied, leaning down to hug her. "We need to celebrate tonight after I close the gallery. What do you say to another cookout on the beach with the three of us, Mom, Erin, and Red if we can steal him away from the Grand Dunes."

"Sure, but what are we celebrating?" Daphne asked.

"Life," he replied, straightening to kiss Hope again. "And love. That's what we're celebrating."

* * * * *

Don't miss the next book in the *Sea Glass Cove* series:

The Driftwood Forts

From a young age, Erin McKinney has been taught that there's only one man she can rely on—her older brother. The rest just aren't worth the trouble. Except maybe Gideon St. Cloud, who is back in Sea Glass Cove to cool off in the middle of a heated custody battle over his son.

Quiet and reserved, Erin is a world away from Gideon's flaky ex-girlfriend and could be exactly what he wants in a woman, but she's wary. In the shelter of her driftwood forts, he'll find out why she distrusts men… and discover how he can prove he isn't like the men who hurt her.

Turn the page to read the first chapter!

One

THE DIP-AND-PULL RHYTHM of paddling the kayak across the ocean on a sultry August afternoon was remarkably soothing. Almost as soothing as the company of man cruising beside her. Erin glanced over at Owen, noted the faint glow of utter contentment that played about his cherished features, and couldn't help but grin in response. His happiness was irresistible and all the more precious for all those months when even a simple smile had been a struggle for him.

"This was a marvelous idea, big brother," she remarked.

"I get them now and again," he replied.

"You ought to work on getting them more often."

It had been far too long since they'd spent all afternoon in the kayaks. The last time had been over three years ago, before a car accident had claimed the lives of her sister-in-law and nephew. Until recently, Owen hadn't been able to drum up the enthusiasm for more than a short trip on Jewel River from the delta to the falls.

"When are Hope and Daphne supposed to be getting back from Montana?" she asked.

"Tomorrow."

"Excited?"

"Don't I look it?"

She eyed him. Excited wasn't the word. Relaxed. That's what he was. "Not yet. You look happy, though." Fondness stirred, and she beamed. "It's good to have you back."

He looked at her, squinting against the brilliance of the setting sun. "Let's not ruin a perfect evening by reminding me of when and why I wasn't so happy, all right?"

"As you wish."

The sun burned orange as it drifted closer to the ocean, and Erin paused in her paddling to bask in the glory of it. It had been unusually hot for the past week, but as day slipped into evening, the air stirred with a hint of a cool sea breeze. She couldn't imagine a more stunning evening to be out kayaking the cove with her brother. They'd paddled all the way down to the southern end of Angel Beach—three miles from home—and were just now passing by Tidewater Point and Otter Island, which divided Angel Beach from Sea Glass Cove. With their unhurried pace, they probably wouldn't reach the northern beach and Owen's truck until after sunset.

Erin started paddling again and steered her kayak toward Owen's, giving him a light bump. He regarded her with a brow lifted and an amused smile. She wiggled her brows. "Race you back to the beach?"

"You want to race the full mile and a quarter?"

"Why not?"

"It's been a while, and we've been paddling all day."

"So?"

"All right." He grinned suddenly, shoved his paddle in the water, and shot ahead with a powerful stroke. "You're on!"

He might have vastly superior upper body strength, but she'd been kayaking a lot more in the last three years, and her strokes were smoother, more efficient, and she had no trouble keeping pace with him as they rounded Glass Island and headed into the pass between it and Stalwart Island. The current flowing around the islands forced her to focus on her task, but the thrill of it coursed through her veins and she let out a crow of pure joy. As they reached the sheltered waters of the cove, she dug in harder and shot ahead.

"Come on, old man!" she called back. "Keep up!"

"Be careful what you wish for, little girl."

The ease with which he matched her pace even though he remained behind her made her nervous. He was toying with her, and as soon as they were within a quarter mile of the northern beach access, he hit the gas and zoomed past her. She scrambled to regain the lead.

Their kayaks slid onto the sandy beach at the same time, and Erin was laughing too hard to crawl out of hers. Owen finally had to offer her a hand up.

"You great big turd," she said, still chuckling. "You played me."

"What?" he asked, grinning. "Did you seriously think I'd lost that much?"

She wrinkled her nose. "Maybe for a minute."

"Gotcha."

"Har har. You're hilarious."

He chuckled. "Come on. Let's get these up to the truck."

Movement at one of the houses on North Point caught her eye, and she glanced up to see a figure stride across the deck of the St. Cloud cottage. From the distance, she couldn't be sure if it was a man or woman. "I thought you said Hope and Daphne weren't going to be back until tomorrow."

"They aren't. She called from her parents just before we headed out in the kayaks. There's no way they could be back yet."

"Then who's that on the deck of the St. Cloud cottage?"

"Gideon must have come out early." Owen frowned. "But just in case, maybe we ought to stop by on our way up to my place."

"I hope it's Gideon."

"Do you now?" Owen teased. "I didn't realize he made such an impression on you when he was here in June."

Erin rolled her eyes, but she didn't dare contradict him because her brother was plenty observant to notice the hitch in her pulse. "What if it's a burglar?"

"We'll tie an anchor to his bootstraps and send him down to meet Davy Jones."

Erin hip-bumped him. "You know, I can't remember the last time you joked around like this. Remind me to thank Hope when she gets home."

They'd made better time across the cove than she'd thought they would, and as they carried the kayaks up the beach and through the sand dunes to the northern parking area, the ruby sun disappeared beneath the waves and the horizon darkened from molten yellow to the deep red of dying coals. Glancing again at the St. Cloud cottage as she strapped herself into the passenger seat of Owen's truck, she thought the SUV in the driveway—which she could see now, from this angle—looked familiar.

"That's Gideon's car, isn't it?"

"Looks like it."

"Guess we won't have to introduce anyone to Davy Jones tonight."

Erin rolled her window down and rested her head far enough over on the head rest to for the wind to cool her face. Hot August nights indeed. Her eyes drifted closed and her lips curved. Right now, in this moment cruising up the highway to North Point Loop with her brother, she was at peace with the world and everything in it.

"Yeah, that's Gideon's car," Owen said.

Without opening her eyes, she felt the truck slow and swerve before coming to a stop, and she guessed Owen had pulled over in front of the St. Cloud cottage.

"I know today was supposed to be a sister-brother day," he said, "but would you mind if I invite Gideon over to join us? He may not be up for it, but it's the neighborly thing to do."

"I guess that'd be all right," Erin replied.

Owen climbed out of the truck, and as soon as his door closed behind him, she lifted her head and watched him stride around to the French doors at the back of the cottage. Why did no one use the front door of this place? Her eyes sought the living room window overlooking the driveway, hoping for a glimpse of Gideon, but the curtains were still drawn.

Owen returned quickly and slid in behind the wheel. "He's going to bring his bags in, and then he'll be over."

"He doesn't want to light the candles first?"

"I didn't ask, but he didn't seem like he was in the mood to do it."

She only nodded, not trusting her voice to hide her intrigue at the prospect of seeing Hope's cousin again. As Owen had pointed out earlier, Gideon *had* made an impression back in June. More of an impression than any man since Chaz.

She sneered. She would *not* taint tonight by thinking of him.

"Hey, what's that look for?" Owen asked. "You want me to go back and rescind the invitation?"

"No," she replied quickly—probably *too* quickly. "That frown wasn't about him."

"Then what was it for?"

She sighed, closed her eyes again, and echoed what he'd said to her by Otter Island. "Let's not ruin tonight with memories of less happy times."

"I'm down with that."

She opened one eye. "What kind of man follows a phrase like 'rescind the invitation' with 'I'm down with that'?"

"One who's trying to erase that sneer from your face."

"Fair enough."

"I've got something I want to show you that'll *really* wipe it off your face," he said, pulling into his driveway. "And I want to show it to you before Gideon comes over, so get your butt out of my truck. We'll get the kayaks later. Or… maybe we'll leave them up there and go out again tomorrow."

"But Hope and Daphne will be home tomorrow."

"We've already planned a barbecue on the beach. Why not take Daph out in the kayaks, too? She hasn't been out in them yet. We could switch off—Hope and Daphne with me and Gideon with you."

Erin groaned. "Don't you dare think about playing matchmaker, Owen. I'm not looking to get involved with anyone. Ever."

"We'll see about that."

"I'm serious, Owen."

"So am I. You spent three years trying to pull me out of the shadows. It's only fair that I return the favor."

"Yeah… and you'll fail just like I did."

With bitterness seeping through her, she stalked ahead of him toward this front door.

"Hey." He grabbed her hand and spun her around to face him. "You didn't fail."

"Didn't I? It took meeting Hope to bring you out of it." Because her voice had a hard edge to it, she stood on her toes and wrapped her arms tightly around his neck. "And that's okay. I don't care what brought you out of it. I'm just glad to see you happy again."

"You ever think that maybe the reason you

couldn't do it was because that part of me never broke?"

"Sure felt like it did."

"I'm sorry, Erin. I never meant to shut you out."

"I know you didn't. Can we stop talking like this? Please?"

"Sorry. But, for the record, I was joking around—sort of. You're the one who took it—"

"All right! You win!" she groaned. "Just show me whatever it is you want me to see. Because the curiosity is killing me."

With a twinkle in his sea-green eyes, he opened the door and held it open for her. Unsure where he wanted her to go, she wandered into his dining room and slid her fingers over the two abalone shells that sat in the middle of his table. The smaller he'd found the day he'd met Sam. The larger had been the sign he'd needed to let go of the past and fully embrace his future with Hope… whatever it might bring. There was a third he'd kept hidden for three years that was now displayed beside his cash register in the Sea Glass Gallery, and she shuddered. The story of how he'd found that one chilled her. So did the fact that he'd kept it to himself until a month ago.

Hugging herself, she looked around and realized he'd disappeared. "Owen?"

"Coming," he called from upstairs.

Moments later, he trotted into the dining room

with a tiny box in hand. Her eyes rounded as he handed it to her. It didn't take too many guesses to figure out what was inside, but even though it was obvious, she inhaled sharply when she opened the box.

Cushioned on midnight blue velvet was one of the most exquisite and unique engagement rings she'd ever seen. It was traditional enough in shape—a smooth band of platinum that flared to embrace a round diamond—but it was what her brother had painstakingly laid into the channels beside the diamond that made it one-of-a-kind. The highly polished, iridescent abalone shell shimmered in the light of the chandelier over his table.

"Oh my God, Owen! This is gorgeous. And you made it entirely yourself?"

"Not entirely, but mostly. I had some help from Hoyt down at Sea Gems. It took me a few tries to get it right. I've never worked with platinum before."

"When are you planning to propose?"

"Don't know yet. I figured I'd give her some time to settle in first."

Erin briefly glanced at him, but her gaze was drawn like a magnet back to the ring. It was so true to her brother and so perfect for Hope that she couldn't find words adequate to describe the pride and joy that swelled in her heart. Finally, she pushed the ring back into the protective velvet and set the box in his palm. She looked up at him. "This is a big deal, Owen."

"Yes, it is."

If she had ever doubted how he felt about Hope, the love that glowed in his eyes right now silenced it. And even as her happiness for her brother threatened to overwhelm her, the old bitterness crept back in. She had no idea what that felt like—that wonderfully consuming bond—but she craved it.

Right then, a knock sounded on the front door, saving her from the inevitable plunge into despair. Her brother jogged to answer it, and her lips curved. How could she be in danger of being lost to that relentless tide tonight? The promise of a bright future full of love and happiness for her brother drowned out everything else.

Moments later, Owen returned with Gideon on his heels, and Erin couldn't help it. She raked her gaze over him with one corner of her mouth lifted in feminine appreciation. With the golden complexion, neatly trimmed anchor goatee and rich, shoulder-length dark hair pulled back in a tail that reminded her a lot of Orlando Bloom's character in the Pirates of the Caribbean movies, Gideon St. Cloud was a more than adequate distraction. And those eyes, so dark and warm…. They threatened to swallow her. His frame and bone structure, lighter than her brother's, might be the product of his St. Cloud genes, but the darker coloring that set him apart from Hope and her daughter was entirely the gift of his Spanish grandmother. Hope's cousin met her gaze with a devilishly charming grin as Owen reintroduced them.

"Gideon, you remember my sister Erin?"

"I do indeed." He took her hand and bowed over it, his grin widening as he pressed a knightly kiss to her knuckles. "*Buenas noches, bonita.*"

"Yes, it is a good evening," she remarked, trying not to snort at his flirtatious greeting. She knew she was pretty enough, but she'd never dream of calling herself a beautiful lady. That description she reserved for her mother, her late sister-in-law, and now Hope. Besides, if she were to give even half a second's thought to his endearment, she'd have to admit how it affected her. "Welcome home to Sea Glass Cove, Gideon."

"Thank you, Erin. This is going to sound really pathetic, but when Owen stopped by and asked if I wanted to join him and you for an evening lemonade…." He shook his head, and there was a weariness in his gaze that had nothing to with his long drive. "You guys make me feel exactly what you said—like I'm coming home. I need that right now."

Whoa. This was nothing like the Gideon she'd met back in June. That Gideon had laughed and cracked joke after joke, seemingly without a care in the world. If she remembered right, it had been over eight months now since he'd broken up with Hannah—he'd called it quits right about the same time Hope's divorce had been finalized. That was plenty of time to adjust to bachelorhood, so why was he worse now than he had been two months ago?

"Where are Liam and your dog?" she asked. "I thought Hope said Liam would be coming out with you."

"That was the plan. Hannah changed it. Again. I left Shadow in the cottage."

The shift in his expression made her uncomfortable, and suddenly, she thought it might be a good idea for her to head home so he and her brother could talk, man-to-man. "I'm sorry," she said quickly. "I should probably go. It's my day to open the restaurant tomorrow, and after our exertions today, I could probably use... the... rest."

The way he looked at her—the blatant plea in those dark eyes—stole the breath from her lungs. What had his ex-girlfriend done now?

"Please don't go," he said quietly.

She was torn. Habits as old as she could remember had her itching to get away, but she couldn't ignore the inexplicable and potent reluctance to disappoint him. She glanced—as she often did—to her brother for reassurance.

"It's not *that* late yet, sis," he replied with a gentleness that belied his casual words.

Narrowing her eyes, she wondered what he was reading into her indecision and skittishness. He knew her better than anyone, but since the accident, he hadn't had the energy or focus or whatever it was that allowed him to sense even the tiniest shifts in her mood, and to see that insightful intensity back in his gaze again now was a jolt. Her heart accelerated, and she wondered how much longer he was going to be satisfied with her vague explanation of why she'd left Chaz.

"Fine," she said with a dramatic exasperation to hide her insecurity. "I'll stay for a bit longer."

"Don't make me twist your arm or anything," Gideon teased.

The return of some of the playfulness that had captured her attention on the summer solstice relieved her and made it easier to reach into her brother's fridge and pull out the pitcher of lemonade. She grabbed three glasses and filled them.

* * * * *

COMING SOON!
For more information, visit:
www.suzieoconnell.com/the-driftwood-forts

About the Author

Suzie O'Connell grew up in Western Washington, but a two week adventure at her stepsister's rustic Montana cabin left a permanent mark, and she has called the mountains and valleys of Southwestern Montana home ever since. She has been writing stories for as long as she can remember, and writes even when she's not writing. Everything around her is story fodder. Her love of writing and of Montana pushed her to pursue (and earn) a Bachelor of Arts in Literature and Writing from the University of Montana-Western.

When she isn't writing, Suzie enjoys spending time in the mountains with her husband Mark, their daughter Maddie, and their golden retriever Reilly. She is almost as happy with a camera in her hand or helping her husband build log furniture as she is writing, and will readily jump on any excuse to enjoy the beauty of Montana.

Sign up for Suzie's newsletter to be notified of new releases and also find more information about her books on her website:

www.suzieoconnell.com

48511660R00124

Made in the USA
San Bernardino, CA
27 April 2017